Besides herself and Ian, there was as yet only one other person in the restaurant. Automatically, Carla eyed him up and down as a potential customer.

"You can forget about him," Ian remarked, reading her thoughts as he attacked a large pizza. "I've already sussed him out. American, but no money. Beach boy type, looking for kicks. You know the type."

"Shhh," warned Carla, stifling a giggle. She stole another furtive glance. Tall, blonde, a bit older than Remo, he wore sunglasses, faded jeans, and an open-necked check shirt, half unbuttoned to reveal a sun-tanned chest glistening with dark golden hair. He had a kind of studied scruffiness about him. A California-style drifter, a straight out of Central Casting. He was leaning back in his chair, very relaxed, and asking Franco, the head waiter, for advice. In fact, he seemed to want advice about every dish on the menu.

Nina Lambert is the author of *A Place in the Sun*, which won the Netta Musket Award for a romantic novel, *Sophie's Story, A Moment to Remember* and *A Rose by Any Other Name*. She started her career as an English teacher in Paris and, after a series of jobs, including positions in advertising, personnel and ecology, she finally settled down to writing as a full-time career. Married to a photographer, Nina lives and works in London.

A Place in
the Sun

A Place in the Sun

Nina Lambert

Woman's Weekly Fiction

A Woman's Weekly Paperback
A PLACE IN THE SUN

First published in Great Britain 1986
by Judy Piatkus (Publishers) Ltd
This edition published 1995
by Woman's Weekly
in association with Mandarin Paperbacks
an imprint of Reed Consumer Books Ltd
Michelin House, 81 Fulham Road, London SW3 6RB
and Auckland, Melbourne, Singapore and Toronto

A CIP catalogue record for this title
is available from the British Library
ISBN 1 86056 000 8

Printed and bound by
HarperCollins Manufacturing, Glasgow

Chapter One

"Jack, darling," purred Helen, catching hold of his arm. "Wait just a minute."

Jack sighed, glancing down at his gold wristwatch. Helen's mania for shopping delayed every appointment.

"Honey," he remonstrated, "we're already a half-hour behind schedule. There's nothing in here you can't get in Bloomingdale's—" His eye was suddenly diverted.

"Exclusive to this store, ladies and gentlemen, and at a special price only while stocks last. Eight fashion blouses in one, eight blouses that fit in your handbag."

A striking, dark-haired girl with impossibly long legs in fishnet tights and a voluptuous figure encased in a pink leotard was holding aloft, between finger and thumb, a small clutch purse.

"As you can see, ladies, I just don't have a *thing* to wear!" the girl continued, looking down at her scanty attire in mock horror. "And I've got a date straight after work! What on earth shall I do?" Her eyes widened in mock despair.

"Let me see." She opened the bag with a flourish and drew out, with an exaggerated air of surprise, something which looked like a folded chiffon scarf. She shook it out like a conjuror, and a gasp went up from the watching crowd which had already doubled in size since her act had begun. Jack moved in closer for a better look, amused.

What followed was five minutes of pure showmanship. Her patter unfaltering, the girl proceeded to convince her audience that they could not survive another day without the Weekender in new Wondercrêpe. Its flowing material was whisked on and off her shapely torso with all the panache of a matador's cape. Belted, unbelted, back to front, inside out, it was transformed by her sleight of hand into an infinitely versatile and flattering garment.

"And so, ladies, here we have eight different styles in one, to match your every mood ... Ideal for holidays ... Keep one ready in your handbag for that unexpected date ... Uncrushable, drip-dry, non-iron ... The Weekender is available in six fashion colours, giving you a grand total of forty-eight variations to suit every occasion."

The crowd was by now itching to buy, but she was not yet ready to receive applause. Not until she had warned them that, due to its fantastic success, the Weekender was in desperately short supply and unavailable in any other store.

"By special arrangement with the manufacturers," the girl announced, her clear, trained voice carrying effortlessly to the back of the throng, "I am able to offer you the Weekender at a discount price for the period of this offer only. But hurry! Stocks are running out and we cannot expect any further deliveries this month, after which the Weekender will revert to its full recommended retail price."

People were already fumbling, agitated, with wallets and chequebooks.

"Jack," wheedled Helen, "I've got to have a couple of those things to take back home. Do you have a charge account here?" she asked vaguely, sifting through her wad of credit cards.

2

"They'll take American Express," he assured her languidly. He'd been caught that way before. No longer impatient, he watched people filing up obediently to pay, Miss Wondercrêpe packing up their purchases with tissue paper and a brilliant smile while two other employees busily took money and account cards. She was on commission all right, thought Jack dryly, as even now she sought to persuade her customers that perhaps they had better buy in more than one colour, while the going was good. Sophisticated black, demure white, dramatic scarlet, sizzling yellow, romantic pink, or delicate blue? Some stalwarts, Helen included, decided to play safe and take all six. The small pile of goodies behind the counter diminished rapidly, investing those at the back of the queue with incipient panic. No doubt there were vast stocks down in the basement, waiting to be brought up in strategic dribs and drabs.

Yes, mused Jack, the girl knew how to sell. An out of work model or actress, he guessed. Dark mahogany hair, honey-coloured skin, liquid brown eyes, and curves in all the right places. She sure wasn't a shop assistant by vocation. He liked her voice, too. Clear, feminine, sexy, one you couldn't help listening to even when, like just now, she was talking utter bull.

He pricked up his ears. She was speaking to a small gaggle of foreign tourists in their own tongue: Italian, fluent. Of course, that accounted for those Mediterranean looks. She was speaking Italian with the ease of one who has learnt it in childhood.

Helen rejoined him with her carrier bag, smiling. "That's a really neat blouse, don't you think? Jack?"

"What? Sure, honey." Jack, it appeared, was no longer in a hurry. Helen followed the direction of his glance, and her lip curled in world-weary amusement.

"We're late, Jack, remember? I thought they had nothing in here you can't get in Bloomingdale's?"

3

Jack laughed his slow, lazy laugh.

"Just professional interest," he assured her, and they went off to find a cab.

"Cor, that was a busy day, Carla," remarked Susie, cashing up her till. "Even for a Saturday. How many did we unload today, then?"

"Fifty-four more than yesterday." The dark-haired girl worked out her commission on a paper bag and entered it in her diary with an air of quiet satisfaction.

"You know, I might buy one myself," mused Susie. "With the staff discount, I might even run to two. The black and the yellow. Or perhaps the pink. Or . . ."

"Don't," Carla advised briskly. "It's gimmicky and badly stitched. A few trips to the launderette and it'll be falling apart. Get something decent in Marks and Spencer instead."

Seven more days of the Weekender in Wondercrêpe and she would definitely have had enough. At least she wouldn't be around to cope with the hassle of people bringing the wretched thing back.

"See you Tuesday, then," said Susie as Carla donned jeans and a teeshirt and flung a faded denim jacket round her shoulders. "Doing anything nice this weekend?"

"Not exactly. I've got an audition on Monday so I'll be spending most of tomorrow preparing for it."

"Ooh," Susie gushed, greatly impressed. "How exciting. Is it for the telly, or what?"

"Theatre – fringe. If I get the part, I'll send you some tickets."

Carla suppressed a smile. She rather doubted if Susie would find the new Josiah Freeman play her kind of entertainment.

Stepping out into Oxford Street, Carla set off at a brisk pace towards Soho, where she rented a bedsitter

4

above the Isola Bella Italian restaurant. Unsalubrious though the area might be, Mamma had felt that Carla would come to no harm living above the Palucchis who, like practically every other Italian family in London, were mysteriously related to her, third cousins by marriage twice removed or something like that. Still, it was thanks to them that Carla had a room in Central London at a rent she could afford, added to which she never risked going hungry. When times were really hard, Carla helped out with waitressing in the restaurant. Provocative in her clinging black dress and white frilly apron, she always got hefty tips and usually ate enough for a week in the kitchens afterwards.

At the moment, despite her labours in Oxford Street, Carla was technically 'resting'. In fact, she had been 'resting' for most of her acting career, although her C.V. made it look otherwise. A scholarship to Drama School, the Siddons Memorial Prize for the most promising student, dozens of parts in far-flung rep, a season with the Bristol Old Vic (where she'd had to learn a grand total of thirty-four lines), a stint of understudying, a medium-size part in a television soap (which had not survived the six-episode pilot run) and the lead in a Channel Four Punk play (in which she had been unrecognisable in chalk-white make-up and purple hair). Then there had been that commercial for chewing gum, a silent close-up of Carla's moving jaws which she felt was best forgotten.

Despite the lack of the proverbial 'big break', Carla had never been on the dole. She had discovered an employment agency, early in her career, which specialised in short-term selling, repping and demonstrating jobs. Cash in hand, no strings, short notice jobs she could drop instantly if any real work turned up. She had sold, in her time, apart from the Wondercrêpe Weekender, advertising space, domestic appliances,

5

insurance, fitted kitchens and electrical components. She preferred, for choice, telephone selling – you could get more done in a day, and you didn't actually have the punters trying to paw you.

Her voice at its most seductive, she would talk her way past draconian secretaries, who thought the call must be a personal one, and lull their harassed bosses into placing orders and granting follow-up appointments for company reps. But she had done the front-line stuff as well, when the expenses and percentages were right, driving company cars and carrying briefcase, samples and rate-books. Jaded executives, expecting a man, had turned to putty in her hands. She talked, they bought. Smiling sweetly, she despised them all. She needed to. The alternative would have been to despise herself.

Carla, a natural idealist, could not have achieved any of this without motivation. She was a hustler from necessity, not from inclination, and had some initial difficulty in reconciling this abuse of her skills with her high-flown, occasionally almost pretentious, dedication to her art. She dreamed of tackling the great classical rôles, admired serious and avant-garde works, and rather turned up her nose at West End potboilers and light-weight sitcoms (not that she would have turned down a part in one). She had the training, the commitment, the professionalism and the talent. But as yet she didn't have the parts. And she needed to eat. More precisely, so did Mamma, Angela, Silvana and Francesca. At least Gabriella now got a grant. But she, Carla, was still the only breadwinner in the large de Luca family. One could hardly expect Mario, who was a priest in the African Bush, to send home more than his blessings which meant that after paying her rent to the Palucchis, setting aside the bare minimum for her own needs and adding, little by little, to a very private nest-egg, Carla handed over the rest of her earnings to Mamma.

"Well, Carla," she would sniff, stuffing the profferred banknotes into her outsize handbag, "if you married Remo, and you won't do better, we wouldn't have to count every penny like this."

Kind, loyal and long-suffering, Remo was shamelessly misrepresented by Carla. "Sorry, I'm engaged," she would say sweetly whenever other men tried to push their luck. Remo, as described by Carla to any male whose attentions proved troublesome, was violently jealous, very large, and prone to Latin outbursts of temper. It was most unfair of her. Remo was in fact good-natured to a fault, trusted her absolutely, and, for all his six foot, wouldn't have harmed a fly. He in no way resembled Carla's convenient fiction of the swarthy, macho piece of beefcake, capable of disposing Mafioso-style of all irksome potential rivals. The ethnic bit could prove useful at times, Carla found. And so she flaunted her sex appeal to smooth her path through life, but no-one ever got to handle the goods.

It was extremely selfish of her, of course, to use Remo in this way and risk eventually breaking the poor fellow's heart. Not that Carla was cold-blooded enough to think of it like that. She told herself that it was his look-out if he wanted to marry her. She had never led him on and perhaps, in the end, she might even go through with it. There was more than one reason why she should, as Mamma never ceased to remind her. Remo, at least, was not an animal. He was caring, generous and kind. He would be the most considerate of husbands. But not yet, she procrastinated. Not until she'd given her career a fighting chance.

She was fast asleep when Remo rang the bell of her bed-sitter at eight o'clock that evening. Exhausted by her efforts of the day, she had lain down on her narrow bed after her shower and dozed off.

Remo was newly shaved, dapper, smelling of Aramis and carrying the inevitable Saturday night bunch of flowers. She greeted him sleepily, putting the bouquet in water and apologising for not being ready. He sat with his back to her while she finished dressing.

"I'd like to have an early night, actually, Remo," explained Carla, clipping on the gold earrings he had given her for her last birthday. "I'm auditioning on Monday for the new Freeman play and I want to spend tomorrow thinking it through."

It had taken all Carla's powers of persuasion to get hold of an illicit copy of the text. Peter Metcalfe, who was to produce, had directed her in the Channel Four play. He rather fancied his chances with Carla as a result of which the unseen passage she would be asked to read would, in her case, be far from unseen. With her photographic memory, Carla would know the part of Anna Price, the tormented heroine of the piece, practically off by heart by Monday.

"What Freeman play?" asked Remo, trying to sound interested. He had spent many a dull hour in the front stalls at the National and the Barbican while Carla had sat, rapt, at his side.

"You may well ask. It's still under wraps. I had inside information on this one. I think I'm in with a chance because I'll be one jump ahead of the rest."

Over a superb meal in the restaurant downstairs, where they were favoured customers, Carla, animated and excited, told Remo all about the Josiah Freeman play. Remo's expression of total attention was not feigned despite his lack of interest in the subject matter. Carla could have recited "Hiawatha" all evening and he would still have listened, fascinated.

Her eyes sparkling, Carla gave him an outline of the plot. Fiercely near the bone, the play had a low-life, inner-city setting and an episodic structure with a commercially disastrous large cast of characters. Freeman, she explained, did not write for the backers or the Saturday matinée audience. The heroine, exploited and abused by men, and degraded by poverty, rose above tragedy, rebelling, fighting and suffering for freedom and self-respect.

It was strong stuff, the best part for a woman in years. Carla was an ardent admirer of Freeman's earlier work, although the same could not, so far, be said for the general public. His two previous plays had generated a good deal of interest from the critics but in box-office terms they had been non-starters. Freeman did not compromise or engage in theatrical politics. He wrote from the soul and lived, it was said, like a hermit, shunning all publicity. He would not allow a single word of his work to be changed or cut. He was already labelled an eccentric. Carla admired all this enormously. Remo wondered how such an arrogant fellow could earn a crust of bread.

"Thank goodness for the Fringe," sighed Carla. "Though I have a hunch this one could make the West End. It's so *powerful*, Remo, so full of . . . of *passion*!"

Watching her spoon cassata into her incredibly kissable mouth, Remo pondered gloomily on just what Carla meant by passion. She was full of fire and spirit all right, but it was all of the mind, not of the flesh. He did not, of course, expect a girl of Carla's innocence to respond to him as certain other ladies did, but he did want to be a faithful husband when the time came. It was not that she was cold with him exactly, in fact he sometimes fancied that he could detect a certain tremor which betokened a holding back, a suppressed desire to let go completely, but despite this he had started to wonder miserably of late if it was not unrealistic to expect her to change overnight into the kind of wife he needed.

"There's a girl who cares only for herself," his mother had warned him repeatedly. "Can you see her giving up her precious career and risking that figure to give you children? Carla de Luca was never cut out for marriage or motherhood."

He bore all his mother's rantings with clenched teeth. Carla could keep her career and her figure if she wanted; he would take her on her terms. But Remo, despite his gentleness, was a man, not a saint. He remained thoughtful throughout the coffee and Sambuccas. Carla looked at her watch – another expensive present from him.

"Do you mind if we call it a night now?" she asked sweetly. "I'm absolutely whacked."

Remo nodded, settling the bill and leaving his usual generous tip. They went outside and round to the side entrance. Carla moved to kiss him good night but he turned her round and followed her up the narrow staircase. Something unfamiliar in his manner forestalled her protests. Perplexed, she let him into the tiny room.

"More coffee?" she asked uncertainly.

"It isn't coffee I want, as you very well know," said Remo quietly. Contrite, Carla put her arms around him and gave him a long, slow kiss. Wretched girl, he thought despite himself, feeling the inevitable stirrings of desire. Doesn't she realise what she's doing to me?

He put his arms round her waist and sat her down next to him on the bed. Predictably, she stiffened slightly.

"Why are you afraid of me, Carla?" he asked, lapsing into Italian. It was always less embarrassing than saying the same things in English. Even her excuses sounded somehow more convincing, and hurt less, when she gave them in Italian.

"I'm not afraid," she murmured, stroking his hair and unconsciously inflaming him further. Her perfume

10

was driving him mad. He drew back.

"Let me stay tonight, Carla."

"No."

"Why not?"

"You know why not," she mumbled awkwardly. She should really have seen this coming.

Remo sighed. "Carla, we're not teenagers. If, as I'm beginning to suspect, you don't really find me – physically attractive, then what sort of marriage can we hope to have?" She couldn't possibly realise, he thought, the pain it cost him to put his fear into words.

Carla, not for the first time, was guilt-stricken. She knew, had known for ages, that she ought either to break if off or give him what he wanted. She knew she was being unfair to him. But, cravenly, she tried stalling.

"I . . . I might get pregnant."

"No you won't. I'll take care of that."

"I thought you were a good Catholic," she prevaricated, playing for time. She didn't like the look in Remo's eye.

"Not that good," he said, smiling wryly. Tenderly, he pushed her back on the bed. He was always tender, always gentle. Carla tried to relax. His request was not, she told herself, unreasonable. She accepted his gifts, his attentions, his protection. She had been sidestepping his proposals of marriage for over four years. She knew that she must seem callous, grasping, unfeeling. Guilt and panic clashed head on. Meanwhile Remo, who had been silently planning this all evening, was already unbuttoning her blouse, kissing her throat, caressing her breasts, murmuring endearments with quiet desperation. He looked into her eyes. His, unlike hers, were totally transparent. Carla could see right through them to the kind, loving, warm man who wanted to make her happy. She hated herself.

He took the intensity of her gaze as implying consent.

11

Hesitantly at first, then more boldly, he began removing her clothes. Numbly, she did not resist. Hardly able to believe his luck, but miserably aware of her tension, Remo tried to soothe her, to arouse her, to tempt her. Was there something wrong with his technique? he wondered anxiously, fighting to keep his own desire under control, mesmerised by the beauty of Carla's honey-coloured body lying there, submissive and rigid with fear under his. Remo had no cause to be so nervous. He was not inexperienced and had never had any difficulties in satisfying other women. He had every reason to believe that he was perfectly competent. She just doesn't love me, he thought, aware that perhaps he should leave well alone. Possibly she would hate him afterwards, refuse to marry him, and then she would have lost for nothing the virginity she so much prized.

Meanwhile, Carla endured her own private torment. You're a bitch, she told herself. A cold, calculating, self-seeking bitch. Don't you think you owe him this much? She tried to relax, to let her body go limp. She tried acting. That helped. He noticed the slackening of tension.

"Are you sure, *carissima*?" he breathed, by now too far gone to heed his nobler instincts.

"I'm sure," she said bravely. She shut her eyes, fighting off remembered images. Remo threw off his remaining clothes. She could feel his hand moving her legs apart. There was no going back, she could not possibly refuse him now. Can a man tell, she wondered absently, if he's really the first? Can he tell if . . .?

There was a sudden loud knocking on the door. They both froze.

"Carla!" shouted Mrs Palucchi cheerfully. "Carla! You awake?"

Remo groaned. Carla, galvanised by the chance of escape, scrambled to her feet and flung on a dressing gown. Remo, sitting defeated on the bed, raised his eyes to heaven and reached resignedly for his shirt. Carla opened the door a fraction and peered out, trying to look sleepy.

"Sorry, Carla, I didn't mean to get you outa bed," Mrs Palucchi said with a grin, holding out a gold earring in her hand. "I find this under your table downstairs. I thought you mighta be looking for it. *Buona notte.*"

Carla muttered her thanks and turned to Remo, her head bowed in shame. He was putting on his shoes.

"Don't go," she found herself saying.

"Forgive me, Carla," said Remo stiffly. "That was all my fault."

She bit her lip.

"Don't apologise," she said. "I'm the one who ought to say I'm sorry. You were quite right, Remo. We ought not to marry. I wouldn't make you happy."

She forced herself to meet his eye. The desolate look on his face tore at her heart.

"Maybe we shouldn't see each other for a few weeks," she continued numbly. "You should go out with other girls. I'm not the only fish in the sea."

"It's you I want, you know that." There was a hardness, a bitterness in his voice she had not heard before. Suddenly yielding to an impulse she had always resisted, Carla blurted: "Remo, perhaps it's time I told you something I've been keeping from you."

"There's another man?" he asked immediately, his worst fears leaping up to meet her confirmation head on.

"No," said Carla, wishing it were as simple as that, her imminent confession giving her a strange sense of giddiness. "But there was, once."

There was a pause.

"You mean," said Remo at last in a strangled voice, "that you still love him, is that it? I don't compare?

13

Tell me!"

"No, I don't still love him. I never did. And in any case, that's all in the past. But I've been deceiving you, Remo." The truth stuck in her throat, choking her. She swallowed hard. "I'm . . . not a virgin."

There was a deathly silence. She had expected shock, interrogation, recriminations. She had just shattered all his illusions, given the lie to all the girlish scruples he had respected so uncomplainingly. But, unpredictably, Remo breathed a sigh of something like relief.

"Is that all?" he finally asked, perplexed.

Carla hesitated. "Isn't it enough?" she asked.

"But why did you lie to me, Carla? Were you afraid I'd stop loving you, darling?"

She avoided his embrace, fiddling with the sash on her dressing gown. Remo drew back, his initial surprise giving way to new doubts.

"Then why," he continued, vexed, "are you so afraid of *me*? Why are you so afraid of . . . of . . . ?"

He had a sudden, horrifying insight. Had some barbarian forced himself on this lovely creature, given her a fear of sex?

"Carla," he asked softly, seizing her hands. "He didn't rape you, did he?"

"No," she replied at length, her voice low with shame. "He didn't rape me. He was gentle and persuasive, just like you. I acted of my own free will. The fact of the matter is, Remo, that I'm well, – frigid. He discovered it, and so would you. You were bound to find out one day. It's not your fault so don't be upset. I hoped it wouldn't be a permanent thing, but it seems like it is. Please don't take it personally."

She faced him boldly, her eyes bright with dishonest candour.

"Darling, Carla, let me –"

"No," she said firmly. "Now I've told you, please

14

don't insult me by trying to 'cure' me. I know it's psychological, but you really can't help. It's best if I don't marry at all. I've been horribly unfair to you, Remo. Please forgive me."

"You mean, you don't want me at all? You really don't like me to touch you? You don't even enjoy it when I kiss you?"

Carla's courage began to fail her. Remo's voice was heavy with a sense of betrayal. She couldn't answer.

"You've been *acting*? With *me*? Why? Did you mean to make a fool of me, Carla?" He gripped hold of her shoulders. "Look at me, damn you!" he almost shouted.

Carla had never seen Remo angry. He had always treated her with such gallantry, such deference, that his sudden outburst, mild by most men's standards, seemed devastating in its suppressed fury.

A clean break, she thought numbly. Kinder for him. Kinder to be really cruel. Placate him now and he'll come back for more. Self-loathing gave her strength. She shrugged convincingly and looked him full in the face.

"I don't actually *mind* when you kiss me or touch me," she said calmly. "I'm pleased if it makes you happy. But, yes, I suppose I'm acting when I pretend to enjoy it. I never made a fool of you, though, Remo. If anything, you're making a fool of yourself, wasting your time on me. Let's part friends now, shall we?"

His eyes had a curious, blind look.

"You're trying to punish me," he stated bleakly, "for trying to get you into bed just now."

"No," said Carla. She took a deep breath. "I meant to go through with it, you know. I felt – sorry for you."

It was, she knew, a huge insult, more effective than a hundred words of reproach or outrage. He recoiled as if she had slapped him.

"I get the message," he said coldly, seizing his jacket

15

and jerking the door open. "Find yourself a new lap-dog!" he called bitterly behind him as he hurtled down the stairs and out into the street.

Carla sat quietly on the bed and tried hard to cry. A good, long, stormy weep was what she needed. But as usual the tears wouldn't come. Carla hadn't cried for years, except on stage. There was nothing but a tight, heaving feeling in her chest, a mixture of pain, guilt and oppression. Despite what it had cost her to make such a confession to Remo, she experienced none of the relief that should have accompanied it. Would she have felt relief if she had told him the truth? And how much had he believed of what she had told him?

No matter, the end in this case justified the means. Remo was not without pride. He could be patient and long-suffering in coaxing a shrinking virgin to passion but he would not risk his self-respect on a shrinking non-virgin who admitted that she remained unmoved by his touch. Innocence and shyness might be seductive, informed frigidity was not. On reflection, she decided, her deception was justified. Remo would be better off without her. And she would have to learn to survive without a protector, without a buffer between her and the enemy.

The nightmares came back with a vengeance that night. Jumbled, surrealistic flashback, the same old images returning to haunt her for the umpteenth time. They were strange, these recurring dreams, in that she knew, the captive of her own tormented slumber, that they *were* only dreams and that she was condemned to suffer them as punishment and must not shirk her penance by waking prematurely. When she did crawl out of the dark into daylight, exhausted, still no tears would come to wash the blood from her wounds. There was no solace to be found in tears. The only escape was in becoming

16

someone else, in donning the mantle of a false identity afforded by her craft.

Shattered, she washed, dressed, did her yoga exercises, and set herself, with borrowed calm, to study "Streetwise", to take upon herself the pain and passion of Anna Price and lose in her the shortcomings of Carla de Luca. The clock ticked on as, sitting cross-legged on her bed, Carla read, studied, and imagined herself into the skin and soul of another person.

How strange, she thought, that it was so much easier to *feel* when you were somebody else. She could never, she knew, surrender herself totally to a man in the manner of the play's heroine. Anna was a creature of fire and sensuality, her electric relationship with her lover charging every page, right through to the dramatic climax where she died at the hands of her jealous and violent husband. Carla who had no husband, no lover, who wished to avoid both eventualities, felt her entire being flooded with borrowed energy from the character she hoped to play. Her heart beat faster, her fists clenched and unclenched, her breath came in gasps as she immersed herself in that other woman's deep and complex relationship with the two men in her life. It was riveting stuff. Give it a Hollywood budget, and a lot of media hype, and it would probably be a blockbuster. As it was, it would be lucky to reach the West End, and even there it would have to fight for its life.

By bedtime, Carla's own personal suffering had been expiated. Exhausted by her mental and emotional exercise, she wept at last for Anna Price and slipped into healing sleep.

Chapter Two

On Monday morning, while Carla waited, heart hammering, to be called for her audition, Jack drove Helen to Heathrow. He paid her excess baggage charge, cursing Wondercrêpe, and headed back in his sleek black BMW to the Knightsbridge offices of Fitzgerald Enterprises International Inc. Leaving the car in the underground car park of the imposing prestige block, he rode up in the lift to the top floor where, unobtrusively, money obeyed his apparently nonchalant command to go forth and multiply.

"Good morning, Laura," he greeted his secretary. "Send the New York office a telex, will you, asking them to send a car to meet Mrs Fitzgerald off PA 239. But first ask Ben to come in."

Laura picked up the internal telephone while Jack sifted through a pile of paperwork, his expression intent.

"Coffee, Ben?" he asked, without looking up as his subordinate arrived, continuing to append his signature to various documents. The casual hospitable query summoned Laura with a tray before Ben had time to answer. Jack sat back and looked across the desk at his newly promoted Leisure Projects Manager. As usual, Ben's face wore the frustration of the workaholic dragged away from his labours. Ben had always found Jack's approach to work infuriatingly cavalier.

"Where are we at with the Catalina project?" queried Jack as Laura poured coffee. "Is it on schedule?"

"Hundreds of applications. I selected fifty for assessment, shortlisted thirty and recruited twelve. That allows for two to drop out. I picked them tough and hungry. Hard-sell merchants with a bit of class. I got the pick. They went for the percentage. Who wouldn't? You could have got them for less, Jack."

"Pay peanuts and you get monkeys working for you," he said with a shrug.

"They're coming in next week for intensive training and briefing before we fly out," Ben continued. "They'll do a good job for you, but I still think we're biting off more than we can chew. We need more time, more manpower, more –"

Jack smiled. Ben bristled.

"I know you don't like risks, but I do. So you won't mind if I take another small one while I'm about it."

He paused, looking at Ben over the rim of his coffee cup. Ben braced himself for a bombshell. Jack always listened politely to his advice. Occasionally, if it suited him, he took it, but more often he did the exact opposite. It was just one of life's maddening quirks that most of Jack's gambles paid off against all the odds.

"I want you to get hold of a girl to join the Catalina team," Jack began, going straight to the point. "I spotted her in action a couple of days ago. She's a natural. Could sell anti-freeze to a snowman."

Ben began shifting around in his chair, looking for a chance to interrupt.

"She's working on the ground floor at Maxwell's in Oxford Street selling a heap of junk called the Wonder-crêpe Weekender. Find out who she is and get her signed up."

"Jack," blustered Ben, agitated. "What's got into you? The sales team is *all men*. And what the hell is a Wondercrêpe Weekender, anyhow? We're not selling novelties here, we're pushing time-share. Sure, I'll have local girls giving out leaflets in the town and on the beach, but we can't have a girl on site! Jack, you told me to get twelve men, hard men with experience, good closers who need the bread. A floozie will upset the apple cart. She'll disrupt the team and won't pull her weight."

"Correction," reproved Jack mildly. "I told you to get me twelve sales people. I never said men."

"Jack, you know as well as I do, women are okay for softening up the market but you need a man to clinch this type of sale. Only a handful of women even applied – all useless. We're asking people to part with a minimum of six thousand dollars in one hit. Wives hate their husbands to buy from a woman, and husbands won't buy if the wife is anti. Jack, you *know* all that. Why?"

"You can't miss her," he continued imperturbably. "About five-eight, dark, well-stacked. Does her act in a leotard and fishnet tights. Even speaks the lingo. Put someone on to it right now. We haven't much time so you'll need to move fast."

Ben smiled cynically. "You can get the girl into bed without putting her on the payroll."

Jack froze him with a look. "I'm not even coming to Catalina, remember? And my bed is my business. No, Ben, she'll be all yours. Look upon it as a challenge."

His eyes returned to the papers on his desk. Defeated, Ben left the office.

Meanwhile, Carla was giving herself up to post-audition euphoria. Her ordeal over, she resolved to live in a fool's paradise until a decision was made. She had, she thought, done reasonably well, although nothing like as well as she could do given direction and proper rehearsal. Shamelessly, she had played up to Peter Metcalfe for all she was worth. Get the part first, she told herself, and cool him off later. She would be a fool not to capitalise on the fact that he obviously found her attractive, even though she knew that she was playing with fire. Good looks could often tip the balance at an audition, and Carla cultivated hers quite cold-bloodedly and without vanity.

She would have much preferred to be a blonde, a cool, Anglo-Saxon English rose, but philosophically she made the most of what she had, if deliberately making the cake so inviting that it seemed sacrilege to cut it. Spectacular good looks, she had discovered, effectively frightened off all but the most confident of men. And even they tended to assume, uneasily, that she must already be spoken for. Her tactics were bound to backfire one day. But until that time came she had a career to forge and a living to earn.

Returning to Soho, she found three notes under her door.

"Ring your Mamma", "Please call in to see Janet", and "Remo phone for you three times. Will ring back" all in Mrs Palucchi's erratic script. Carla felt the beginnings of a headache building up behind her eyes. Picking up her purse, she went to the payphone in the hall.

"Mamma? It's Carla."

Mrs de Luca grunted explosively, and a flood of rapid, agitated Italian poured down the telephone. In summary, Mamma had just had the final demand for the electricity and the piano tuner had discovered rampant woodworm. Not only would they soon be using candles, it seemed, but Silvana's musical future was doomed. Carla let her rant on. She threw in for good measure that Francesca's feet were becoming stunted for lack of new shoes. She would grow up with feet like a China-woman. Etc, etc, etc.

22

Carla, from long experience, let her mother exhaust herself before replying, soothingly, that she was calling in at the agency for her money that day and would send her a cheque for the electricity and the shoes. The piano was a bigger problem. Wondercrêpe commission wouldn't run to a new piano.

Mrs de Luca was somewhat appeased, however, and snorted her thanks in the usual oblique manner which always made Carla feel guiltier than ever. The headache was beginning to take a grip when, mercifully, the tension was broken by Francesca taking over the phone.

The sun came out. Francesca didn't mention new shoes. Francesca just wanted to tell Carla her latest childish doings, prattling gaily in a strange mixture of the two languages she spoke with equal facility. By the time the pips went, Carla was smiling. Still worried about Silvana's piano, but smiling nonetheless.

"Well, well, well," teased Janet, of the Salespower Agency, counting out ten-pound notes and giving Carla a receipt to sign. "Who's been headhunted, then?"

Carla, absorbed in mental arithmetic, didn't react at first.

"Headhunted?" she asked vaguely. "Someone's asked for me specially?"

"And how," smirked Janet, pulling Carla's dossier out of her desk drawer. "And a nice fat fee for me, too, if you play ball like a good girl."

Carla sat down, intrigued.

"Ever heard of Fitzgerald Enterprises?" asked Janet. Carla hadn't.

"What's the deal, Jan? As it happens, I'm skint. All this lot is spent already. I need something quickly and I can't face much more of Wondercrêpe."

Janet became businesslike. She had known Carla for a long time now and had made a lot of money out of her. But she wasn't sure if Carla would take this particular bait. Three months abroad might interfere with her love life, not to mention her acting ambitions. Actors were all alike, she had several on the books. The Equity minimum was always more enticing than any amount of sales commission.

"Fitzgerald Enterprises are into property. Multinational stuff. Buy land, build on it, sell it. Very diversified. Offices, shops, hotels, you name it. This is small beer for them but a great chance for you. They've just bought out a residential operation in Tuscany. Holiday villas and apartments, half-built when the money ran out – some local entrepreneur got out of his depth. Fitzgerald stepped in and made a takeover bid. They've restarted the building and now they're sending in a sales team to offload the apartments on a time-share basis to tourists. Time-share's the big new thing – people buy a week or more of holiday accommodation per year for life. That way every unit sells for much more than its individual worth. Lots of profit for Mr Fitzgerald and lots of lovely commission for you."

Carla pondered. "How exactly did they get my name?" she asked, puzzled. "Have I worked for one of their subsidiaries or something?"

Janet shrugged. "Seems they heard you could sell," she replied succinctly. "Word gets round, you know. Then, of course, you speak the language which gives you an advantage." She looked at her watch. "They want to see you as soon as possible. Feel like an interview?" Her hand was already on the phone.

"Any idea what a piano costs?" asked Carla abstractedly.

"A piano?" echoed Janet.

"Uh-huh."

"Haven't a clue. But if you want one, you'd better let me make this call, hadn't you?"

And five minutes later Carla was on her way to Knightsbridge.

Plush offices, she noticed, looking round the understated splendour of the reception area: leather chairs, thick grey carpet, and white hessian walls. She wasn't really dressed for an interview, she was dressed for Peter Metcalfe in a rather revealing low-cut black teeshirt and very tight jeans. She looked casual, provocative, sexy, a bit too bohemian for this sort of place. For an interview she would have chosen to look businesslike but persuasive in a tried and trusted clinging jersey two-piece.

She shrugged dismissively. For some reason, Janet seemed to think this job was as good as hers. And a few months abroad might not be a bad idea, with the Remo situation as it was. She hadn't the energy or the will power to keep dodging him, and plainly she could not have done him enough damage on Saturday for him to be leaving telephone messages for her again already. Quite apart from all that, acting jobs were thin on the ground in the summer. Even supposing she got to play Anna Price, "Streetwise" wasn't due to start rehearsals until the autumn.

Lost in thought, she came to with a start as a smartly dressed secretary came out and said that Mr Holmes would see her now. She noticed the girl looking her up and down with a certain fascination, which unnerved her slightly. Interviews, she reminded herself, were a doddle compared to auditions. She wasn't exactly nervous but she had an uneasy feeling, as the secretary and Mr Holmes exchanged glances, that she was an object of some speculation.

"Please sit down, Miss de Luca," Ben invited curtly, offering her a cigarette, which she declined, and lighting one for himself. The ashtray, Carla noted, was brimming. Rather florid and harassed in his shirt-sleeves,

25

Ben was the prototype hard-pressed sales manager, a battery of telephones on his desk jostling for space with the inevitable framed photographs of his kids. Carla knew the type.

Trust Jack, Ben was thinking, shutting his lighter back into his drawer. This girl was a looker all right. Involuntarily, his eyes wandered over her. Used to this, Carla remained unmoved and looked back at him impassively.

Fantastic high cheekbones, he noted, and eyes so dark you could drown in them. Forcing himself to ignore her neckline, Ben began speaking rather fast.

"Miss de Luca, as you already know, we decided to approach you on the basis of your sales record to date. Your agency tell me you've had very diverse experience, and that you've been consistently successful. Now, we happen to have an opening in this company for a really dynamic sales person, to promote a product you can really believe in ..."

Carla had heard this kind of spiel countless times before. Selling inspired an almost religious fervour in professionals like Ben Holmes. Words like commitment, motivation, sincerity, achievement, targets and incentives fell from his lips in a torrent of conviction. She let it all wash over her until he mentioned money. The figures he quoted made her catch her breath. That would certainly put her in the market for a piano.

"The rewards are high, but the challenge is unique," he went on, moving on to the more practical details. Accommodation and full board would be provided on site, he explained, and a subsistence allowance would be paid weekly, with net commission being paid direct into a UK bank account at the end of the contract. The pace would be fast and the pressure intense, he warned. Only people with the most extensive and proven track records were being selected for this undertaking.

26

"How big is the sales team?" she enquired, imagining it to be Armada-like.

"If you join us, you'd be the thirteenth," said Ben, experiencing a stab of superstition. "Mr Fitzgerald believes that a small team engenders friendly competitiveness, and gives everyone a bigger slice of the cake. This is the company's first venture into this type of market. If it's repeated, successful personnel will be approached again."

He lit another cigarette. How cool this girl was, he thought irritably, while Carla, inwardly quite excited, looked suitably sceptical.

"Does that mean you're officially offering me the job?" she asked innocently, as if it were all the same to her. It never paid to look too keen.

Ben swallowed his annoyance. He'd had people falling all over themselves to get on this team, had selected, pruned and re-selected to pick only the ones with the enthusiasm, skill and guts that guaranteed success. Ben took his work very seriously indeed. It rankled with him to be told by Jack to recruit this girl on spec, just because she'd turned him on demonstrating some nonsensical female knick-knack in a department store, so much so that it had positively galled him to hear Janet's well-documented account of Carla's previous sales experience. It always riled him when Jack's instincts were vindicated.

"Young lady," he said with asperity, "I *am* officially offering you the job. But you might as well know you are something of an afterthought. I had already recruited my team when Mr Fitzgerald asked me to see you. You're his choice, as it happens, not mine. It worries me, quite frankly, that you would appear to lack staying power with any one product. Your career record is erratic, patchy. I've no room for dilettantes on this project, Miss de Luca, and if you accept the position it will be conditional on your participating fully in the training programme here in London next week. Perhaps I shouldn't be telling you this, but I'm taking you on under orders."

There, he had got it off his chest.

"Supposing I turn down the job?" parried Carla, stung. She had a sudden perverse desire to take the invisible, presumptuous Mr Fitzgerald down a peg or two.

Ben took a deep breath. Damn the woman, she was going to play hard to get. He would have the devil of a job convincing Jack that he hadn't deliberately put her off. Maybe he had. He looked hard at Carla, playing poker.

"Miss de Luca, you would be looking a gift horse in the mouth," he countered dryly, "but personally I don't give a – don't care whether you turn it down or not."

There was a pause.

"Okay. You win," she said at length, massaging his ego with a brilliant smile. Relieved, Ben smiled back. She was a tough cookie all right, but she was hooked.

Filling in forms with his secretary afterwards, Carla discreetly pumped her for information. She found, to her surprise and relief, that she would have no direct contact with the mysterious Mr Fitzgerald who, it seemed, was based at company headquarters in New York, although he visited London with the frequency of a commuter. Fitzgerald Enterprises, explained Laura, were moving into Europe in a big way. Efficiently, she took down Carla's personal details, and handed her a folder full of sales material in preparation for the coming week's training programme.

She wondered if Ben had warned Carla that she would be the only woman. Not that it would worry Miss de Luca, thought Laura dryly. The girl looked as if she

28

could take care of herself.

"What did you think of her?" she asked Ben after Carla had left. He raised his eyes skyward.

"Jack and his harebrain schemes," he grunted. "Can you imagine the effect a broad like that will have on twelve guys? I can't make him out."

"You know Jack," Laura reminded him, "he believes in hunches."

"I had this operation all sewn up," Ben complained. His heartburn was bothering him again. "Offer Jack good odds on a sure thing, and what does he do? He goes off and backs an outsider."

"Yes," laughed Laura. "And he usually wins."

The prospect of going to Tuscany for the summer blunted Carla's disappointment at failing the audition. She had been close, very close, Peter Metcalfe had assured her, but the part had gone to an up-and-coming TV actress who looked more likely to attract West End backing.

But he was only saying that to spare her pride, Carla told herself. She just hadn't been good enough, and that was that. For the hundredth time she wondered if she wasn't kidding herself, whether she shouldn't knuckle under and accept Mamma's relentless advice that she should get a 'proper job'. The prospect of escaping her dilemma for a while, justified by such lucrative fringe benefits, seemed all the more enticing.

Eventually, she had had to take a call from Remo, reasoning that if she didn't he would be more likely to confront her in person. It was a sticky conversation with Remo sounding very unhappy. He was upset, he said, at the way they had parted. He wanted to remain friends. Carla didn't know if she could face the constant reproach of Remo's continuing friendship just yet. It was a good thing for both of them that she was going abroad. He could seek pastures new while she was away, and it would look as if their relationship had just petered out during her absence which would be less damaging to his pride, and less provocative of speculation, than if they had just suddenly announced their break-up. There would be no frenzy from her Mamma, and no gloating from his.

As it was, Mamma didn't argue once she heard about the money to be made, and had been assured that of course Remo did not object to Carla's going to Italy.

"Tuscany," she had said cryptically, "is a long way from Naples. Much too far for you to have time to visit . . . any of the family."

Carla looked at her mother and got the unspoken message.

"Much too far," she agreed.

The sales training programme was held in a London hotel, Ben presiding. It was very slick stuff. The first day, a film was shown depicting the area of Tuscany coastline around Catalina, as yet a minor resort still ripe for development. There followed a slide show depicting the layout and location of the complex, and illustrating the different sizes and types of villa and apartment on offer. Fitzgerald architects, surveyors, and interior designers had been flown out to assess what had obviously been a very haphazard operation, and knock it into shape quickly. Although building work continued it was unobtrusive and leisure facilities, such as pool, tennis courts and restaurant, were already functional.

Ben was good at generating product enthusiasm. Even Carla, who generally had no feeling for what she sold, found herself admiring the evident attention to detail that appeared to be a hallmark of Fitzgerald company policy. The object of the exercise might be to make a profit, but expenditure was not stinted and high standards had been set to ensure that every purchaser got his moneysworth.

Lunch was provided in the hotel restaurant, and a very good lunch at that. It was good psychology, of course. The prospective sales personnel, faced with a top-class menu, felt duly appreciated and began to identify themselves with the stylish, high-flying, Fitzgerald empire. The conversation over the meal was animated shop talk. Ben was well pleased. Jack had allowed a generous budget for this programme, saying that it was a good investment. By the end of the week, people would be itching to get out there and sell.

Carla, much to Ben's surprise, was quickly accepted as one of the gang. The scope of her selling experience enabled her to join in with the conversation easily. She knew all the jargon, and had had employers in common with several of her new colleagues. Such an unexpectedly decorative member in their midst boosted team morale in the most subtle way. Never mind that she was the only woman, and a stunningly attractive one at that, she knew her stuff. At this rate, mused Ben, watching Carla laugh and joke in a totally non-flirtatious way, she would end up as company mascot.

Carla, chameleon-like, was instinctively able to adapt herself to her new rôle to her own best advantage. By integrating herself with the group as a whole, by being open and friendly with all of them, she aimed to keep male territorialism at bay. Effectively they would all protect her against each other. Carla needed sexual harassment like a hole in the head. She was joining this venture to make a lot of money quickly, and she wanted no unwelcome amorous attentions to divert her energies from achieving that goal.

On day two, the principles of time-share were explained. The Catalina complex would be computer-

31

linked to other developments all over the world, allowing owners to swap their weeks in the sun with counterparts elsewhere. Dull details of costing criteria, service charges, and price variation were explained lucidly with audio-visual aids. It was all-important, Ben told them, that they should understand the principles and structure of the scheme if they were to be fully confident and knowledgeable when selling the product.

By the middle of the week, they were on to the real nitty-gritty of making people buy. Lists of consumer questions were drawn up and answers to every conceivable objection were rehearsed.

"If you don't sign the prospect up there and then," pronounced Ben, "you've lost the sale. People who say they'll think about it *never come back*. And you don't get a second chance, because you can't go to them."

A man appeared suddenly with a video camera. Ben licked his lips.

"Now," he continued, his eyes scanning the room, "Laura and I are a pair of tourists. We've got the money, but we know it all. We'll object to everything you say and we won't buy without a struggle. Who'll take us on?"

He looked round for a victim, eyes gleaming sadistically, until they fixed, inevitably, on Carla. He beckoned her with a finger. A subdued hum of sympathetic laughter emanated from her male counterparts. No-one liked to be the first to make a fool of himself on close-circuit television.

"Come on now, don't be shy," cajoled Ben. He still felt he had something of a score to settle with Carla. The girl was too damn cool for her own good. She was a natural scenestealer. He would show her who was boss.

Laura, who had rehearsed the rôle of the carping wife with Ben earlier that day, experienced a stab of sisterly sympathy for Carla. She felt that Ben ought to have picked on one of the tougher, more experienced men to break the ice. Quaking inwardly, Carla rose apparently unperturbed. Her trained memory had already enabled her to learn the sales pitch off by heart and she knew the answers to every objection as well as she knew her catechism. Realising that her credibility as a saleswoman was now on the line, she rose to the occasion.

That video tape, at Jack's command, was kept for years afterwards as a training classic. Carla needed only one take. Word perfect, she never missed a cue. She was used to thinking on her feet. She had had to ad lib her way out of all kinds of trouble in rep when other people dried or fluffed their lines, when props were missing, doors jammed, or bits of scenery toppled over. She was a professional down to her fingertips. She tied Ben up in knots in the most courteous and civilised way. By the time she had finished with him, he had a choice of signing on the dotted line, or appearing a complete eunuch.

Laura, to Ben's fury, actually started siding with Carla against him. Useless to try to explain to him afterwards that this had not been collusion, that Carla had manipulated her as well. For the sake of Ben's bruised ego, he needed to believe that Carla and Laura had been in cahoots. A burst of wild applause greeted Ben's defeated signing. Carla smiled ruefully. She would still rather have been playing Anna Price.

After that, she was recruited to replace Laura in the rôle of the wife while her colleagues tried to sell to Ben. Inspired by her example, they performed the rest of the exercise with enthusiasm, eager to emulate the standard of quick-witted confidence that she had set them. When the extracts of the tapes were re-run later, Ben commentating on body language, pointing out unconscious mannerisms and mercilessly freezing the picture to highlight where people had gone wrong, Carla was still the most obvious Oscar nominee. No-one could now regard her as the project's 'token woman'. She had earned her spurs.

Jack Fitzgerald himself was conspicuous by his absence. Catalina was Ben's baby, and Jack's theories about delegation precluded stealing his thunder. For all his outward brashness, Ben's ego was a delicate flower, and at this early stage he would have felt quickly upstaged by Jack's inescapable charisma. Jack's Midas touch with money stemmed from his amazing gift for handling people. While never letting anyone forget who was boss, he allowed all his executives almost unlimited freedom and responsibility. He didn't keep a dog and bark himself. Ben alone would get the glory if Catalina went well, and for all he had said repeatedly that it was a high-risk operation, he had a personal stake in its success.

"Relax, Ben," soothed Jack, as the project manager chain-smoked his way through dinner the night before the group's departure for Italy. "You've picked a good team. I saw the tapes. They've done their homework. Rehearsals are over, there's no more you can do. Get a good night's sleep – you look shattered."

Ben was a good man but he lived on his nerves too much, thought Jack, especially since his recent divorce. He missed his children and he hadn't stopped licking his wounds. A change of scenery would do him good.

Ben picked at his food dispiritedly. That damned indigestion was getting worse. He fumbled for his antacid pills.

"Jack," he said, shaking his head and sighing, "don't you ever worry? Don't you ever wake up at night in a cold sweat? Don't you ever fear failure?"

34

It was a theme that had always fascinated him. Jack could have invested his money in certainties and retired by now. He could have owned property outright, in his own name, all over the world. He could have bought himself financial security for life. Instead, perversely, he lived out of suitcases and used all his profits to finance further ventures. He borrowed heavily against all his collateral. One bad decision, one major error of judgment, and Jack, as an individual, could be ruined.

Jack sat back and smiled his familiar slow, enigmatic smile.

"Nope," he shrugged. "I worry more about success than I do about failure. Success makes you fat and lazy and complacent. It's all come too easy for me, I guess. So I like to keep myself on my toes. Risks keep me wide awake in the daytime. That way I sleep better at night."

Ben shook his head, mystified. Jack was a law unto himself. He didn't crave the security an ordinary man needed. At thirty-four he had still not married. Indeed, his relationships with women were a source of endless speculation, especially his relationship with his sister-in-law Helen.

Since Jack's younger brother had been killed in a flying accident a couple of years earlier, Helen had been, quite unashamedly, working hard at ensnaring Jack. It was common knowledge that he stayed at her apartment in New York, and that they shared a hotel suite when she visited London. But that didn't prevent Jack picking up other women, apparently with Helen's full knowledge. Subterfuge was not his style. On one memorable occasion, Helen had flown into London unexpectedly, and Jack, a red-headed model in tow, had cheerfully suggested a *dîner-à-trois*. What he had done come nightfall Ben dreaded to think, but somehow he had managed to remain on excellent terms with both ladies.

Everything Jack did was effortless. He had nerves of steel. He didn't smoke, drink, or go to an analyst. He was unmoved by fast cars and fast living. A weakness for women appeared to be his only vice, but even in that he remained in control. It would take some woman to get the better of Jack. With something like a pang of envy, Ben pondered how good it would be for Jack to meet a woman who didn't fall straight into bed with him. Success made you lazy and complacent, he had said. He was lazy and complacent about women all right. He'd never had to climb a tree for his plums. He just shook it gently and they tumbled, ripe and willing, into his hands.

"You were right," admitted Ben, his thoughts still on women, "about Carla de Luca. She can sell."

"Have you found out yet what else she can do?" teased Jack.

"You've got to be kidding. That girl wears a large 'keep off' sign. The guys all make a fuss of her, but no-one's got lucky. She's so damn *friendly* no one can get near her."

Jack nodded. "Sounds like good technique. She'll save her sex appeal for selling. A girl with those looks doesn't need the hassle of in-house admirers."

"She certainly seems to know how to look after herself," said Ben. "They say those Italian chicks tend to have a hell of a temper. Push it with her, and I reckon you could end up with a black eye. Pity you're not coming with us, Jack. You might find you've met your match."

Jack laughed good-naturedly. He was contemplating an energetic evening with his most recent conquest, an air stewardess he'd met on his last Concorde trip. That girl sure knew how to fly.

"Be my guest, Ben," he said generously. "It's time

36

you took up a hobby. And it's a lot better for your health than jogging."

Ben coloured, and resolved to lose a bit of weight.

Carla was anxious not to drop out of circulation altogether as far as 'real work' was concerned. She rang her agent, Molly, to inform her of her trip.

"I'll come back straight away if anything worth while crops up," she told her, "but I just can't afford to jack this job in unless it's for a decent part."

Molly, who smoked cigars and swore like a trooper, wrote down the Catalina address in purple felt tip pen and snorted.

"A part is a part is a part," she chanted, a favourite saying of hers. "If you want to get fussy, there are plenty of others waiting in the wings. I thought you were supposed to have that Freeman play in the bag, Carla."

Her voice was heavy with reproach. Carla seethed inwardly. She had got that audition without any help whatsoever from Molly. Like all actors, her relationship with her agent was strictly love–hate.

"What are you selling this time?" Molly continued. "Spaghetti?"

"Time-share," Carla replied sullenly. She was always on the defensive with Molly on the subject of her off-stage activities. "Matinées every day, but at least it's a three-month run. And I had more lines to learn than *you* ever got me."

"Cheeky," Molly returned good-humouredly. "Break a leg, love," and she rang off. The theatrical code-phrase for 'good luck'. Carla had a feeling she would need it.

She spent her last day at home with her family. Gabriella was back from college, and was about, through Carla's good offices, to commence a vacation job in the china department of Maxwell's in Oxford Street.

"Remo's giving me a lift into town every morning," she enthused, "so I don't have to worry about fares. And he's told the Buon Appetito in Brewer Street to give me whatever I want for lunch!"

The Buon Appetito was the newest addition to Remo's fast-growing chain of delicatessans. Carla smiled uncomfortably. His generosity to her family always made her feel guilty, especially now when she had hurt him so badly.

"Won't he miss you dreadfully, Carla?" asked Gabby. "Doesn't he mind you going?"

Carla gulped. No-one knew of their recent rift.

"I expect he'll survive," she answered evasively. "Why don't you look after him for me?"

Gabby chortled gaily. She looked amazingly like her elder sister when she laughed. Although she was taller, thinner and less obviously striking than Carla, she had a vivacious sense of humour and an extrovert personality. The two girls had always been very close.

"Remo's adorable," she conceded mischievously, "but he doesn't approve of my views: thinks women are strictly for keeping house and having babies. I shall bombard him daily with women's lib until he's begging for mercy."

It had always mystified Carla how Mamma would listen indulgently when Gabby ranted on about politics and feminism. If only Mamma would start nagging Gabby about marriage for a change, it might take the heat off me, she thought ruefully.

"Remo is a good boy," pronounced Mamma for the hundredth time. "Carla don't know when she's well off. You get back from Italy, you name the day. He will wait for you, Carla, though the good Lord knows you don't deserve it."

She bit off a piece of cotton between her teeth.

"Gabby, she's got brains. Gabby can manage without a man. Carla, she needs a husband."

She flung her eldest daughter a meaningful glance, and Carla looked away.

Chapter Three

Carla had never worked so hard in her life as she did that first week in Catalina. Tourists, bribed by promises of free local champagne by promoters patrolling the village and hotels, flocked to the development.

She soon learned to sort out the sheep from the goats and not to waste time on the 'sightseers', those who had neither the means nor the intention of buying and had come just for the perks. A sixth sense enabled her to spot and cultivate likely purchasers. Minor details of dress and appearance betrayed their income bracket, and their answers to a few well-aimed, casual questions revealed the true level of their interest.

Time was money. You couldn't hope to clinch a sale in less than an hour, or to close more than one sale in four, on a good day. So some people got a bare ten minutes from her before she politely left them to their own devices. But to one large, prosperous American family, she devoted nearly a whole day, driving them round the area and taking them to lunch at her own expense. Her instincts paid off triumphantly. They bought three high-season months of a four-bedroomed villa outright. Ben kissed her. Everyone queued up to kiss her. Her success set the ball rolling, acting as a huge incentive to the rest of the team.

After the first exhausting fortnight, Carla had already

earned, on paper, enough for Silvana's piano. Jack Fitz-gerald certainly believed in rewarding hard work. Her slice of the action was more than generous, and she felt dizzy working out how much she might earn if she managed to keep this up. She hoped that her initial success wouldn't prove to be a flash in the pan.

Her earnings were, furthermore, all net profit. It cost her practically nothing to live at Catalina. A two-roomed apartment in the complex was provided, meals were free at the on-site trattoria, and a local car-hire firm supplied transport at the company's expense. Carla drew virtually none of her subsistence allowance in order to leave her final commission free from deduc-tions. She evaded invitations, and went to bed early to sleep off the rigours of the day. She wanted to keep herself to herself and avoid the complications of socialis-ing with her male colleagues.

On the third Monday morning sales meeting, a beam-ing Ben, gesturing enthusiastically with a lighted cigar-ette, informed them all that they were well ahead of target. A huge wall chart showed the weeks and units already sold, blocked out in different colours represent-ing the various successful sales persons. Red and indigo predominated. Red was Carla. Indigo was a forceful, hardliving Glaswegian called Ian McIntyre. Ian took selling very seriously and was extremely put out that Carla was fractionally ahead of him. It was only because of that freaky American deal, he was quick to point out to her over coffee. He'd actually closed more sales than she had.

Carla didn't argue. She was more than happy to ack-nowledge him as star of the show, and reassured him accordingly. She didn't want to fall out with Ian McIn-tyre, or anyone else for that matter. In fact, she didn't want anything to upset her equilibrium, what with every-thing going so well. She was therefore extra sweet to

Ian, to the point of humbly asking his advice. Men, she found, simply loved that. Ian proved to be no exception. He softened, and expounded his theories to her attentive ear. Privately he was thinking, not for the first time, that this girl would be quite a catch. Anyone who succeeded in scoring with Carla de Luca would be undisputed king of the castle.

Carla, relieved to have kept resentment at bay, rather overdid her little woman act and left Ian feeling quite devastatingly macho. Before dismissing the group, Ben announced that, subject to the third week's sales exceeding the second, there would be a celebratory champagne party on the following Saturday night. Then everyone went off to do battle.

Left alone, Ben reached for his bottle of Bismuth. That Italian food, delicious though it was, didn't seem to agree with him. He swallowed a spoonful of the white liquid, screwing up his face, and put through a call to London. He badly wanted Jack to fly out and see for himself what had been achieved so far. The targets Jack had set had been impossible, ridiculous, and yet they had exceeded them. He wanted to show off. He wanted a pat on the back. Now he had proved himself, he wanted, for some inadmissible reason, Jack's reassuring presence. Because, deep down, Ben was scared.

"Terrific," came Jack's languid tones over the wires. "But I knew you could do it, Ben. You sound kind of uptight. Is there a problem?"

"I think I'm getting a bug," said Ben feebly. "The food's a bit rich – all that olive oil. Jack, how about coming out next weekend to see for yourself? I'm throwing the guys a party if they keep up output, which they will. I'd like you to be there."

"Guys? What about the girl?" came the amused query.

"She's making out. Sells hard and lives like a nun.

43

But it's early days. These high-flyers haven't always got stamina, they can burn themselves out. And there are one or two at the bottom of the league who may drop out. It's survival of the fittest." Ben winced again. "Well, can you make it?"

Jack caught the note of urgency in Ben's voice. Catalina was strictly Ben's party and he would not voluntarily have gatecrashed it.

"Sure, if you want me to," he confirmed casually, careful not to betray a growing suspicion that all was not well. "I'll aim to get there early and have a look around, incognito. I might spot any weak areas that way."

"Fine," Ben agreed. "Have a meal in the restaurant while you're at it. There's something peculiar about the food."

"I'll do that," promised Jack. "See you, Ben. Take it easy."

The third week took its toll on Carla with the perpetual strain of beating her own record. Anxiously, she watched the little red squares form a random pattern on the huge sales chart. But for once, she actually believed in her product. She might have considered, had she had the means, buying a piece of Catalina for herself. Her apartment overlooked the glittering pool with distant views out to sea. Every fixture and fitting, the carpets and soft furnishings, spoke of taste and quality. The grounds were imaginatively landscaped, with a feeling for the local environment; the atmosphere in the complex was one of luxury, peace and relaxation. The surrounding countryside was unspoilt and idyllic, and she wished she had more free time to enjoy it. Her growing attachment to the place generated a real enthusiasm, far more convincing than that which she simulated for Wondercrêpe and allied merchandise.

Technically, Carla worked a five-day week, but in

practice, the complex being open daily, she never allowed herself a day off. There was too much at stake, she was too acutely aware of how much she was earning, and the difference which so much money could make to her future plans. She wondered what she would do if Molly recalled her to London with a tempting offer. All the more reason to make as much as possible while the going was good.

By Friday evening, Ben was able to confirm that the champagne party would go ahead. Targets had been maintained, despite the sudden departure of the least successful team member, and spirits were high. The next day, Carla was lunching on her own in the trattoria when Ian McIntyre, flush from a big sale, swaggered in and sat down at her table. Carla, who never ate breakfast, always had her midday meal early and usually ate alone. Besides herself and Ian, there was as yet only one other person in the restaurant. Automatically, Carla eyed him up and down as a potential customer.

"You can forget about him," Ian remarked, reading her thoughts as he attacked a large pizza. "I've already sussed him out. American, but no money. Beach boy type, looking for kicks. You know the type."

"Shhh," warned Carla, stifling a giggle. She stole another furtive glance. Tall, blonde, a bit older than Remo, he wore sunglasses, faded jeans, and an open-necked check shirt, half unbuttoned to reveal a suntanned chest glistening with dark gold hair. He had a kind of studied scruffiness about him. A California-style drifter, straight out of Central Casting. He was leaning back in his chair, very relaxed, and asking Franco, the head waiter, for advice. In fact, he seemed to want advice about every dish on the menu.

Franco, proud of the choice on offer, described each option in succulent detail, and encouraged him to try the *Risotto Milanese al Funghi* when he could have

45

pushed something more expensive. Carla smiled to herself. Franco was passionate in his enthusiasm for the trattoria, in which, like all the resident staff, he had a share of the profits.

"Carla, you're not listening to me," complained Ian McIntyre. She switched her attention to him with a start.

"Sorry, Ian, what were you saying?"

"I said, can I partner you to the party tonight?" he repeated patiently. Carla, unprepared, was cornered.

"Partner me? Well, I mean, we'll both be there anyway, won't we? It's just a company thing."

"Ben's thrown it open to everyone connected with the complex. All the leafleters will be there, the domestics, the builders, and the local bureaucrats." His eyes gleamed. "I could keep the wolves at bay for you, Carla. Stop anyone getting fresh, pinching your bottom, that sort of thing."

Carla wasn't all that keen on parties of any sort. It was hard to stop men groping when they'd had a few drinks. Ian grinned.

"Well? Will you let me fight off all the hopeful Romeos? There are more of them about than you might think. Come on, Carla. A party's no place for a wee lassie on her own."

Carla laughed, joining in the joke. There was more than a shred of truth in what he said. Besides, Ian was all right. Like her, he was only interested in his commission.

"Okay, then," she said, smiling. Ian smirked to himself. First base. That would be one in the eye for the other lads. He looked at his watch. Ian always ate on the run. He would end up with an ulcer like Ben. Mission accomplished, he made a speedy exit.

Carla, wondering whether to indulge her weakness for pistachio ice cream, returned her attention to the solitary diner. A perplexed Franco was being told that

46

the risotto was not to his taste. Carla watched, fascinated. The risotto was always excellent. Creamy and fragrant, it was one of the restaurant's specialities. Franco, volatile by nature, would go up in smoke.

With a superhuman effort, however, he nodded heavily at his guest and bore the offending item back to the kitchen, returning a few minutes later with a seafood platter in its place. His patience was further tried when the American asked for each crustacean to be individually identified. Franco's zeal slowly reasserted itself as the stranger sampled each variety in turn and expressed his approval. Franco's polite stiffness gradually softened into beaming satisfaction, and further words were exchanged sotto voce. Carla saw Franco glance in her direction, then cross over towards her table.

He bent over and whispered, close to her ear, in rapid, conspiratorial Italian: "The American gentleman wonders if you would care to join him for dessert and coffee? You saw the bastard send back the risotto. Do me a favour, Carla. Make him buy, huh?"

She hesitated, remembering what Ian had said. Still, he could have been mistaken. What a laugh it would be to prove him wrong and pull off a sale. Maybe the American was an eccentric millionaire in disguise. He had a certain unorthodox style about him, might just be worth a try ... And if it was a simple pick-up, she would shake him off pronto.

Graciously, Carla crossed the restaurant and offered the American her hand. He rose and took off the tinted glasses to reveal eyes of a startling Adriatic blue. He had finished the shellfish, and asked her advice about the sweets.

"Pistachio ice cream," she counselled unhesitatingly. "They make it on the premises. I'm surprised you sent back the risotto," she added boldly. "It's usually very

47

good."

He smiled quizzically. "You eat here often?"

"Every day," she confirmed, accepting a glass of wine. "I work here, selling the apartments. You won't mind, will you, if I try to sell one to you?"

This forthright approach, the only feasible one in her view, quite took him by surprise. He surveyed her with frank amazement.

"You shoot a very straight line, lady," he commented mockingly, "but I'm afraid I'm just a no-good beach bum. Down to my last cent."

He had evidently, as Carla had feared, overheard Ian's indiscreet remarks. Well, she decided, even if he was speaking the truth, she might as well finish her lunch at leisure. Rushing food brought her out in spots. She always gave herself a full hour at midday.

"I hope you've got enough to pay for the meal," she continued, undaunted. "You were lucky Franco didn't challenge you to pistols at dawn. The risotto is his pride and joy. I don't fancy your chances with him if you can't settle the bill. But actually," she ventured archly, "I think you're a millionaire in disguise."

His eyes opened wide again, a slight tremor disturbing his deadpan expression. He looked down at his faded denims.

"Either it's my Savile Row suit," he drawled, "or you spotted me arriving in the Rolls. But even if I were a millionaire," he added provocatively, "I wouldn't throw my money away on what you're selling."

Carla bristled at the ill-informed contempt in his voice. Sending back the food and now knocking the apartments! The man was a complete peasant. She turned on her sweetest smile. Insolently, his eyes ranged slowly over her. She met his gaze unwaveringly until the ice cream arrived and they took simultaneous delicious mouthfuls.

"Is it nice?" she asked unnecessarily.

"Superb," he replied, looking at her breasts. Carla blinked.

"If I was right about the ice cream," she remarked coolly, "perhaps I'm right about the apartments too."

It was cat and mouse after that. One minute he would listen, question, and appear impressed by her answers; the next he would raise all manner of tricky objections. It was hard work. The swine turned out to know more about time-share than she did. But, increasingly, she was sure that this man had money. Never mind his scruffy attire, everything else about him betokened power, confidence, success.

The restaurant filled up and emptied again. They drank more coffee. He drew her away from her subject, and she lured him back on to it again. Eventually, choosing her moment carefully, she invited him to look round an apartment. The timing of this was always crucial. Don't bring on the dancing girls too early, as Ben was fond of saying. The build-up had to be just right.

"I thought you'd never ask," he said cryptically, rising from the table. Carla gave him the guided tour: the pool, the sports facilities, the gardens, the views, the beach, and last of all an apartment. Optimistically, she had led him up to the most expensive one on offer, the penthouse. A vast living area with expensive leather furniture, three bedrooms, all with en suite bathrooms, and a balcony the size of her Soho bedsit.

She continued to field his innumerable awkward questions while sitting on the penthouse verandah sipping cold drinks from the apartment fridge. His manner veered unpredictably from the businesslike to the suggestive. Figuratively, he sent back the risotto and re-ordered it half a dozen times.

Finally he said, "Okay, honey, you win."

Carla held her breath. He grinned broadly.

"Honest to God," he continued, "you've sold me. I'd sign on the dotted line right this minute, if I hadn't bought the lot already. I was right about you. You're dynamite, Miss de Luca."

Carla was horrorstruck. There was a painful pause while several pennies dropped noisily and her brain whirred round like a fruit machine. She had not told this man her name but, obliquely, he had just told her his. The man who had told Ben Holmes to take her on, for reasons she still didn't know. A man who had just put her through her paces like a circus pony. Feeling utterly foolish, she adopted a smile of bright sophistication.

"How do you do," she said, "Mr Fitzgerald."

How absurd he had made her look, she thought furiously, tinkling out a brittle little laugh to hide her confusion. She would claim she had guessed all along, of course, and given him a run for his money. But even as she drew breath to say so, Jack Fitzgerald leaned over her chair, pulled her to her feet, and kissed her.

He had the advantage of surprise. Carla, despite her radar-like early warning system, had not seen this coming. Totally unprepared, she had the choice of struggling or submitting, but not, as she usually did, of taking evasive action. Struggling seemed undignified, and in this case futile. Dumbly, without responding, dazed and shocked, she let the kiss continue.

Remo would never have dared a kiss like this. A kiss so suggestive, so self-assured, so uncompromising, as to leave her in no doubt whatsoever as to what was in his mind. It was terrifying in its explicitness. By the time he released her, she was shaking, her eyes full of fear and defiance.

Jack paused, perplexed. Carla slapped his face, hard, and marched off.

He put a hand up to his stinging cheek and gave a

long, low whistle.

"Atta*girl*," he said.

Carla shut herself safely inside her own apartment and began busily justifying her own behaviour. He had had no right to kiss her like that, to assume a proprietorial *droit de seigneur*, to humiliate her as he had done. But he was, unfortunately, the boss round these parts, like it or not, and she could have repelled his unwanted attentions without resorting to physical violence.

She had over-reacted. Her Latin temperament, her natural tendency to dramatise everything, had overruled diplomacy and level-headedness. A girl with any sense would have exploited the situation, she told herself, instead of inviting the sack.

Her face flooded with feverish colour as she remembered the utter powerlessness she had felt as his mouth had covered hers, provoking, exploring, pillaging. His kiss had betrayed the supreme sexual arrogance of a man who regarded any woman as his for the taking, who did not pause to consider her feelings in the matter, who took her ultimate surrender for granted. She shuddered and told herself she was glad she had slapped him, and that she would not hesitate to do so again. Not that the occasion would arise a second time. He would have got the message loud and clear, and his pride would surely not risk a repeat performance. On reflection, she decided he was unlikely to retaliate by firing her. Not with her sales record.

Increasingly, Jack was worried about Ben. Closeted in his office with him that afternoon, surrounded by charts, figures and graphs, he noticed the manager's grey complexion, clammy skin, and the way he chain-chewed antacid tablets.

"You're overworking again, Ben," he observed

51

mildly. "And you're smoking too much. Why not take a break? The place can run itself for a few days."

"No way," Ben responded automatically. "Not yet. It'd be asking for trouble. You ought to know, Jack, salespeople are like fast cars – they need a speed cop on their tail, to stop them crashing into each other and running over pedestrians. It's getting very competitive and a few of them – McIntyre for one – have to be watched or too much stuff will go off the books post-sale. A couple of people have signed up just to get him off their backs, and have withdrawn later. It gets the place a bad name."

Jack picked up the telephone.

"You're going to have a check-up," he announced calmly. "Today. If necessary, I'll take over for a few days while you have a rest. I'll knock McIntyre into shape for you."

Ben snatched back the phone.

"No, Jack," he protested irritably. "If you're trying to ease me out . . ."

Jack sighed. Ben was ultra-defensive about his territory. He didn't want to offload responsibility, but he wouldn't risk sharing any credit either. Ben was afraid that a few days of Jack's sitting in his chair would destroy his credibility with the sales staff, but he was in trouble, thought Jack, or he surely wouldn't have asked his boss to make this unscheduled visit.

Tactfully, Jack continued, "Of course I'm not trying to ease you out. Who the hell would I replace you with? You've been in on this project from the beginning. I just want you to do something about that pain."

"I promise you I'll see a local medico on Monday. You don't call up a doctor at the weekend, not unless you're dying. And then there's the party tonight. I'm okay. It's just the food. I told you, it doesn't agree with me."

"The food is excellent," retorted Jack. "And the service. I played merry hell in the restaurant at lunchtime, sending stuff back and giving Franco the third degree. He didn't turn a hair. I've just been back there to have a word with him, look round the kitchens, meet the staff and so on. They were quite relieved my complaints hadn't been for real, those guys really take a pride in their work. No, it's not the food, Ben. Have you started an ulcer?"

"For God's sake!" Ben exploded. "Don't nag! I've had enough nagging to last me a lifetime, remember?"

The reference to his unhappy marriage was unmistakable. Shrugging, Jack changed the subject.

On reflection, Carla was glad that she had agreed to let Ian McIntyre escort her to the party that night. She was less than ecstatic at the prospect of confronting Jack Fitzgerald again, especially in a social setting, and it would be reassuring to have Ian protectively at her side. She guessed, accurately, that Ian probably wouldn't stray far all evening, and at the moment that suited her just fine. It wasn't as if she would be giving him any encouragement and, knowing Ian, after tonight he would start looking for easier pickings among the local talent. Ian was a go-getter and liked quick results. Ian was no Remo.

Three weeks of constant sunshine had tanned Carla's natural honey colour to a burnished gold. Her simple, sophisticated black dress was starkly effective against her tawny colouring, her low-cut neckline offset by several heavy gold chains – all presents from Remo – glinting tantalisingly against her smooth skin. It was paradoxical that Carla maximised her looks, exploited their effect, and then ran for cover. Beauty was power, she had discovered. It gave her a weapon. It was currency. But it was also dangerous, a two-edged sword.

The party was to be held in the trattoria, the tables rearranged around its perimeter to leave space for a small dance floor.

Ian looked like a cat who had got the cream, arriving with Carla on his arm. At her apartment door he had kissed her decorously on the cheek, eyes flying to her cleavage, and told her that she looked beautiful. She had smiled graciously, unmoved, a girl who got compliments every day of the week.

No point pussy-footing around with a woman like that, decided Ian. He would behave himself till he took her home and then move in for the kill. He would lay money that underneath that cool exterior she was red hot. But first, he thought, get her nicely tanked up, just to help things along. Smiling, he offered her a glass of champagne.

A delicious buffet of antipasti was laid out on a large table, and the guests were already making cheerful inroads into this while Franco and his staff looked on benignly. Carla didn't recognise most of the throng as she had few dealings with the armies of non-sales people involved in the complex. Waves of the old, innate shyness washed over her but she trod water bravely, shaking hands and producing polite conversation to order. Ian was soon very much involved in earnest shop talk. He had a tendency to dominate any group and hold forth at the drop of a hat. Carla listened passively, looking suitably impressed.

Surprisingly, she had discovered, Ian didn't – or wouldn't – dance. When her limbs began twitching to the insistent beat of the music, she had tentatively suggested that they join the other couples on the dance floor, but he had declined, saying, "Sorry, Carla, but I'm not much of a one for dancing," meaning, she suspected, that he had no sense of rhythm and couldn't bear to be seen not excelling at anything. Just as well, she reflected. He would soon be unsteady on his feet, judging by the amount of champagne he was putting away. Unknown to her, he had also been surreptitiously refilling her own glass rather more often than she would have wished, but she had been too busy evading Jack Fitzgerald to notice.

She had spotted him almost immediately, looking devastating in a white suit, circulating among his guests with Ben hovering at his side. Ben's skin looked positively green in this artificial light, contrasting gruesomely with Jack's healthy tan. As yet, they had not made it as far as Carla's end of the room, but they were approaching relentlessly, moving from table to table and shaking hands with everyone from the site architect to the cleaners. It was a very democratic gathering, and people of all ranks were lapping up the Fitzgerald charm like ice cream. It was Jack's increasing proximity that had driven her to try to inveigle Ian on to the dance floor, careless of the dangers of inviting such close physical contact. She was nervously draining what she imagined to be her third glass of champagne when she felt a tap on her shoulder. Too late for escape. It was Ben.

"Jack Fitzgerald, Carla de Luca," he recited unnecessarily. "Carla's doing a great job for us here," he admitted nobly. "Aren't you, Carla?"

Jack Fitzgerald gave nothing away. He shook her hand gravely and looked at her steadily. He didn't smile. Neither did Carla.

"Time for a break, I think, Ben," he observed at length. "Will you do me the honour?" he asked, with mock gallantry, indicating the dance floor. The jungle beat had been superceded by a slow, smoochy number. Carla hesitated, but he was already leading her firmly by the elbow. Unwilling to appear at all put out, she had little choice but to follow obediently. She bent her head so that her hair fell forward to conceal her hot cheeks. He put his arms around her waist, leaving her no option but to place hers on his shoulders. The difference in their heights gave her a good view of a pale blue shirt and silk tie. She shut her eyes, which served only to enhance her other senses. He smelt delicious, subtly masculine. He felt, as they moved slowly to the music, warm, sinewy, and dangerous, exuding controlled energy as he guided her slowly around the floor. His voice was soft, low and vibrant. She already knew what he tasted like.

"I wanted to apologise," he was saying, without a hint of remorse, "for jumping on you today. My only defence is that I did look before I leapt. Looking at you turns out to be a dangerous pastime, as I discovered."

Carla opened her eyes and cleared her throat nervously.

"Apology accepted. I'm sorry, too. I shouldn't have slapped you, but you gave me a fright." Oh dear, she could have put that better.

"I guess I'll take that as a compliment, intended or not. Tell me, how do you like Catalina? Better than Maxwell's?"

Oh my God, thought Carla, *that* was where he had noticed her. Prancing around like a chorus girl in that ridiculous outfit. No wonder Ben had been anti. She gasped, and pursed her lips to hide her embarrassment.

"Catalina," she confirmed pertly, "is definitely better. I hope you didn't get the wrong idea about me. Wondercrêpe was all a bit come-into-the-kasbah, I'm afraid. I can assure you I don't wear a leotard to sell the apartments."

"Just as well," observed Jack, "or we'd soon have a riot on our hands."

Carla blushed, glad of the dim lighting, hoping that

the music would stop soon, wishing it wouldn't.

"It's hardly that kind of pitch," she remarked, lapsing into sales-speak. "Basically, it's the wife you have to sell to, remember? Normally, you know, I wouldn't try to close a man on his own. In your case, I guessed from the start who you were. I just thought I'd play along to prove what a hard worker I am."

"Of course," he conceded, amused, seeing right through her. "And I knew you knew. So I had to make it tough for you, like I did for Franco. I'm here on a fault-finding mission, but it was hardly necessary. Everything seems to be going like clockwork. Ben's a perfectionist. That's why he's in charge."

"He overworks," said Carla bluntly, without thinking. She'd met so many Bens before. "And he worries all the time. He never seems to relax."

"He's goal-oriented," corrected Jack.

"Goal-oriented? How *American*!" she blurted, finding the jargon dehumanising. Goal-oriented? Killing himself, more like.

"How *Italian*!" was the counter-thrust. "What a volatile little signorina you are. Anyhow, what exactly do you mean, 'How American'? I'm a mixture of at least four nationalities, probably more, and I live out of a suitcase. That makes me a citizen-of-all-the-world. American for short."

He shot her a lazy, well-practised smile as, to her relief, the music stopped.

"I'd better return you to lover-boy," he mocked, noticing a glowering Ian McIntyre out of the corner of his eye. It was a pity, he mused, that he would be leaving so soon. Thank goodness, thought Carla, that he wasn't staying long.

She was preoccupied for the rest of the evening. She danced with several of her colleagues, eyes clouded and far away, and abstractedly drank, with Ian's connivance, far more of the cold, fizzy wine than was good for her. Too late, she realised that the room had begun to revolve around her and that she felt rather sick. Carla never got drunk. She hated to feel out of control and one memorable hangover in her student days had inoculated her against further excesses. But now she was miserably aware that a combination of stress and heat had driven her to treat the champagne as a thirst-quenching, nerve-steadying beverage which, alas, it was not.

She tapped Ian on the arm. His face, too, was rather flushed, although from long practice he could hold his drink far better than she.

"Ian," she hissed quietly, "I'd like to go to bed now. I'm very tired. You stay if you're enjoying it. Good night."

"No, no," he insisted, all effusive, if overblown, gallantry. "I'll walk you back." His speech was very slightly slurred, the effects of the alcohol causing him to revert to the guttural accents of his childhood.

When they got out into the cool evening air, Carla realised just how far she had exceeded her capacity. Her knees gave way, and had it not been for Ian's steadying grasp, she would have fallen over in the most undignified fashion. He needed no more encouragement to put his arm around her shoulders while she leaned against him gratefully, clutching the waistband of his trousers for support.

"Oh dear," she giggled apologetically, hiccupping. "I'm afraid I've had a bit too much to drink."

Ian grinned reassuringly and helped her to open the door of her apartment.

"G-goodnight, Ian," mumbled Carla, her head spinning. "Thank you for bringing me home." He seemed quite dauntingly sober in comparison to herself, although in fact he was anything but.

"What you need," Ian said smoothly, "is some strong black coffee. And so," he added purposefully, "do I." He shepherded her through the doorway, following closely. "You just make yourself comfortable. I'll get it."

Carla sank weakly on to the divan in the living area. She would sleep on it in her clothes, she decided vaguely. She was too tired to move. She closed her eyes but the room immediately started to sway again, the divan a miserable fishing boat bobbing on waves of nausea. She opened her eyes to quell the sick feeling. Perhaps coffee wasn't such a bad idea.

"Kettle won't take long to boil," announced Ian, cheerful with anticipation. He sat down next to her and pulled her head against his shoulder.

"Sleepy?" he murmured.

"Yes, very," she confirmed, trying to focus. Ian appeared to have two faces, superimposed haphazardly one upon the other. The effect was grotesque. She blinked, stiffening as his hand began massaging her arm insistently.

"Why don't you have a lie down?" he suggested cosily, lifting her legs on to his lap and rearranging cushions.

Carla shook her head. She didn't like to admit how sick she felt. Lying down would be fatal. Deciding it was time she visited the bathroom, she attempted to get up, but Ian pulled her down again.

"Whassa matter?" he enquired thickly. "Give us a wee kiss, Carla."

And then, before she could prevent him, he trapped her lips in a wet, wobbly, messy kiss. Carla, repelled, kept her mouth firmly shut and pushed him away.

"Please, Ian," she wheedled, not wanting any bad feeling. "I'm tired and we're both tipsy."

Ignoring her protest, he carried right on kissing her, his hands running up and down her back, his tongue forcing her lips apart, slippery and unwelcome in her mouth.

"Ian!" she spluttered, gasping for breath. "Please stop it!"

Already worked up and heedless of her objections, he began pulling down the zipper of her dress, dragging her down on top of him. She squirmed violently and, absurdly, they both rolled on to the floor in a heap so that Carla, dress half off, lay pinned down by his full weight. She wriggled, dreading an unholy scene.

"Get off me this minute," she choked, fighting for calm against mounting panic, "or I'll scream!"

But he just laughed in the most lascivious manner and proceeded to make screaming an impossibility with another stifling, frenzied kiss, obscene in its uninvited intimacy. Carla began banging at his back and sides with her fists to no avail, increasingly frightened now as she realised, from the urgent pressure of his body, just how aroused he was.

Fear shot adrenalin through her veins and sharpened her dazed wits. Strategically, in desperation, she stopped struggling and went completely limp. Complacently, Ian released her momentarily to begin throwing off his clothes. Seizing her opportunity, in a split second Carla had twisted free of him and grabbed hold of a heavy glass ashtray from the coffee table.

"Get out," she shouted, angry now, raising her arm as if to strike him with it. "You're disgusting!"

Ian stood up and swayed slightly.

"Don't give me all that," he muttered, undeterred, advancing on her. "You're screaming for it, any fool can see that. Don't be a tease, Carla. You want it as much as I do."

He caught hold of her arm.

"I don't 'want it'! And if I did, I certainly wouldn't want it with you!" stormed Carla, her breath ragged with terror. Ian was a big, burly man, far too strong for her to resist. A mixture of alcohol and lust made him impervious to pleas or reason.

"Stop playing hard to get," he sneered knowingly, unbuttoning his shirt. "Or do you like to play rough, Carla? Is that what turns you on? You want to fight me, is that it? That's fine by me. Sounds like fun. Let's fight, baby."

His leer turned her stomach. Horrified, she watched him unzip his trousers. She darted for the door. He made a lunge to stop her and, galvanised by terror, she crashed the glass ashtray against his forehead with every ounce of strength she possessed.

Stunned, he fell to the ground like a stone and lay in a crumpled heap at her feet.

For a moment, Carla stood paralysed with horror at what she had done. Then, as a red trickle oozed from his head on to the pale carpet, she realised, her heart thumping painfully, that she must get help. Oh God, suppose she had killed him?

Scrambling back into her dress, Carla rushed off into the night, knowing that she had no choice but to return to the party and report her crime to Ben. She visualised police, ambulances, Ian's funeral, herself in the dock, Mamma and the girls pale in the public gallery.

Running, head down, through the landscaped gardens towards the trattoria, sobbing with panic, she collided suddenly with something very solid. It was Jack Fitzgerald, taking the air. He caught hold of her by the shoulders and halted her flight.

"What in hell is the matter?" he demanded, taking in her haggard face and dishevelled appearance.

Carla, panting to get her words out, could only stammer: "Must tell Ben. It's Ian, he's had an . . . accident."

"Show me," commanded Jack. Wildly, she turned and ran back the way she had come, wishing desperately that she would soon wake up and find that this had all been a hideous nightmare.

Jack took charge immediately. He didn't comment at the sight of Ian's inert body but knelt to take his pulse, peering under his eyelids and hauling him into a sitting position before slapping him briskly and repeatedly on both cheeks.

"Should you move him like that?" she asked fearfully, dubious about this rough and ready treatment.

"Lady, I spent two years in the Marines. I learned to tell the difference between dead and dead drunk. If he hadn't been half-cut he would have hit you back, instead of keeling over."

He looked at the ashtray, still lying where she had dropped it, and picked it up speculatively.

"Just as well you're weak and feeble," he commented, "or you could *kill* someone like that. Looks like I got off lightly. What did the poor bastard do to you?"

Ian was grunting now and beginning to blink. Jack handed Carla a key.

"Go to my apartment, 314, and bring back the brandy you'll find in the kitchen."

Number 314 was four doors along. Trembling, Carla did as she was bidden, returning with a litre bottle of duty free Remy Martin. By this time Ian, head between his knees, was groaning theatrically.

"That wee wildcat," he was protesting, "I didnae hardly touch her."

Jack shot Carla a meaningful look as she handed him the brandy and a glass.

"Drink this, man," he said calmly, "and then go and sleep it off."

Ian gratefully accepted a hair of the dog and then, unsteadily, got to his feet and allowed Jack and a chastened Carla to help him to his apartment where they left him spreadeagled and dazed on his bed, removing his shoes and covering him with a quilt. In token of his restored health, he promptly passed out again and began snoring loudly.

"You next, madam," said Jack firmly. Grasping her arm, he frogmarched her back to her rooms and shut the door behind them.

"Do whatever you have to do in the bathroom," he instructed her, "and then get into bed. You should take some Alka-Selzer or something. You're going to feel rough in the morning."

She instantly succumbed to the effects of shock. The last hectic fifteen minutes since she had fought off Ian had imbued her with artificial energy. Now, it drained from her. Her body began to shudder convulsively, her legs buckled beneath her. Worst of all, the room began spinning with a vengeance.

She did not make it to the bathroom in time. As Jack shot out an arm to steady her and take her weight, she was violently, spectacularly sick, all over his immaculate blue shirt.

He didn't flinch but picked her up and carried her into the bathroom, propped her up against the wash-basin, and ran the taps while she retched and heaved, convinced that she was in her death throes and only vaguely aware of his supporting arms. When the spasms ceased, exhausted, she allowed him gently to wipe her face with a damp flannel. Bliss! The room had stopped moving, the nausea had passed. Her head, however, was beginning to hammer viciously. She opened her eyes and winced as she saw the state of his shirt. It was not a pretty sight. Registering her distress, he immediately unbuttoned it and dropped it carelessly into the bath along with a very sodden tie.

"Better now?" he asked kindly. Carla, horribly ashamed of herself, blushed at the sudden intimacy of having Jack Fitzgerald, her employer, a man she hardly knew, alone with her at midnight, bare-chested in her bathroom.

"Turn round," he commanded, and, unbidden, unzipped her dress for her. "Clean your teeth and you'll feel better. Then get into bed. I'll come and tuck you up." There was just a hint of gentle mockery in his voice.

Dumbly, she obeyed. She could hear him moving about in the kitchen as she climbed gratefully into bed. She had the oddest feeling of safety, of pleasant drowsiness, despite her recent ordeals. He knocked before entering her bedroom, and handed her a large tumbler of water.

"Drink it all or you'll be dehydrated in the morning. That's what actually causes hangovers, you know," he remarked conversationally. He sat watching her swallow. It didn't seem nearly as outlandish as it should have done to have him sitting there shirtless on her bed, his bright blue eyes looking straight through her thin nightgown. Shyly, she averted her eyes from his muscular arms and broad chest, and concentrated very hard on drinking the water.

"Good girl," he said approvingly, accepting the empty glass. "Now go to sleep."

He pulled the covers round her and gave her a chaste kiss on the forehead. For just a split second, something stirred deep in Carla's subconscious. But before she could identify it, she slithered into sleep.

Chapter Four

Carla slept heavily but woke early to be greeted immediately by a merciless technicolor action replay of the events of the night before. Groaning, she staggered out of bed to swallow a couple of hasty aspirins before retrieving Jack's battle-stained shirt from the bathtub and immersing it in hot soapy water. The silk tie, alas, was beyond redemption and she was forced to consign it to the bin.

The shirt was of thin, almost transparent cotton lawn with a Jermyn Street label inside the collar. No doubt he bought them by the dozen, but it had become inordinately important to the fastidious Carla to restore it to him, pristine and unmarked, as soon as possible. She left it to soak while she had a shower, rubbed at it energetically, rinsed it repeatedly, and then rolled the fine fabric between two towels until it was damp dry. She pressed it with care, hung it up to air, and resolutely forced herself to do her yoga exercises and drink some orange juice and instant coffee. She was just contemplating how exactly she would set about tactfully returning his property to him when her phone rang with the double bleep which denoted an internal call. Gingerly, she picked it up.

"Eight-thirty," the voice drawled. "Rise and shine. Come and have some breakfast."

"I've been up for ages," she retorted crisply. "And I don't eat breakfast. I'm afraid I had to throw your tie away, but I've laundered your shirt. Can I bring it over now?"

"You can even put it on me," he chuckled, hanging up.

Let's get this over with, she thought, seizing the shirt and marching along to number 314 where the door stood ajar. Jack Fitzgerald, wearing a towelling robe, hair still damp from the shower, was nonchalantly stroking an electric razor over his chin. The smell of percolating coffee was tantalising, as was the scent from a bowlful of huge ripe peaches.

"Thank you," he said briefly, taking the shirt from her. "Help yourself to coffee."

He disappeared into the bedroom, to return moments later wearing jeans and a teeshirt. She could understand why Ian had written him off. He looked too laid-back, too easy-going, too young, too impossibly casual to be a moneyed tourist, let alone the head of a multi-million dollar empire.

He pulled a chair out for her. A breakfast tray was laden with fresh rolls, butter, honey and juice. He must have sent down for it to the trattoria kitchens. He poured them both coffee and began attacking a roll with a healthy appetite as if, for all the world, it was normal for them to share breakfast together like an old married couple.

"Feeling better?" he queried, reaching for the honey pot.

"Yes, thank you," said Carla sheepishly. "Do you think Ian will be all right?"

"Don't worry about him. I went and hauled him out of bed just before I rang you and stuck him under a nice cold shower. He's a new man. And pretty terrified of you, I might add. Kept telling me you were a regular

66

spitfire, he never laid a finger on you, etc, etc, etc. He's got a filthy headache, though. And a bump on his head the size of an egg. Going to tell me what really happened?"

His eyes fixed on hers, inviting straight speaking. Carla invariably either embroidered on the truth or edited it. It had become a defensive, almost automatic habit. But it seemed unworthy not to level with Jack Fitzgerald. He had an air of all-knowingness which discouraged falsehood.

"He made a pass, started tearing my clothes off. He was drunk and he thought I was teasing when I said no. I panicked."

"So why did you take him back to your room in the first place?" enquired Jack mildly. "To see your etchings?"

Carla flinched. "He said he wanted coffee," she admitted, feeling foolish.

"Of course. 'Coffee' usually means sex, you should have found that out by now. How old are you? Fifteen?"

Carla coloured. "I know, I know. But I didn't think – I'd had too much wine without realising it, and I thought coffee might sober me up. I didn't think Ian would –"

"Well you should have thought," stated Jack flatly. "You don't go to a party in a low-cut dress, wiggling your little butt the way you do, and not expect any man, given half a chance, to try to score."

"I do *not* wiggle my . . . er, butt!"

"Yes you do. You probably can't help it. Don't worry about it, it's irresistible. Along with a couple of other things." He took a big bite of roll and deftly quartered a peach, handing her a segment, dripping with juice, so that she was obliged to eat it quickly.

"I can't make you out," continued Jack chattily. "You gift wrap the package like crazy and then get sore if

67

anyone tries to untie the ribbon. Use brown paper and Scotch tape in future, it's a helluva lot safer. I can see now I got off with a warning. McIntyre was lucky there wasn't a meat axe lying around."

Carla, her mouth full of peach, was unable to comment.

"You know, you're quite a challenge, Miss de Luca," he continued wickedly, reaching over with his napkin to wipe the peach juice off her chin. "*The Times* crossword's got nothing on you. Pity I'm flying home tomorrow, or I could have some fun working out all your clues."

Carla stood up.

"Thank you for the coffee, Mr Fitzgerald," she said stiffly. "But I think it's time I wiggled my little butt off to work. Sunday happens to be our busiest day."

"Hey," said Jack, putting out an arm to stop her. "Don't get mad. I thought we were pals."

Confused, she looked away. It was hard to come over all haughty with a man who'd looked after you while you brought up your dinner. Undaunted by her frosty expression, he gave her a special and very private smile. She blushed and smiled back ruefully, defeated.

"Thanks for the advice, pal," she said. "I'll be more careful in future."

"You do that," said Jack Fitzgerald, and with mock formality shook her hand, leaving her feeling a strange mixture of relief and disappointment.

"Goodbye then," she mumbled, "have a good flight," and she hurried from the room.

Carla went straight down to the office to complete her paperwork for the previous week's sales before the first potential clients started to arrive. She was immersed in figures and calculations when one of the chambermaids accosted her in some agitation. Carla was well known to the domestic staff as being Italian speaking,

68

and often translated as necessary. Rosa was explaining volubly that there was something the matter with Mr Holmes. Because he was always an early riser, his was the first apartment on the daily worksheet. The maid had let herself in as usual at nine o'clock to find him still in bed and looking extremely ill. He had told her to go away, but he had sounded very weak. She felt bound to cover herself by reporting the matter. It was common knowledge that Ben had not been well. Perhaps, suggested Rosa, he needed a doctor.

Unhesitatingly, Carla accepted Rosa's master key, went with her to Ben's apartment, and knocked sharply on the door. When there was no response, she took a deep breath and let herself in.

Ben was lying, half-dressed, on top of the bed. His face was grey and he was pressing his hands to his chest, his eyes full of fear. He appeared unable to speak, and was breathing with obvious difficulty. With a sudden, sickening thud of recognition, Carla's mind flew back to Pappa, lying in intensive care, all those years ago. Sitting behind the screens, with Mamma weeping and the priest intoning, Carla had, at her mother's insistence, seen her father die. Ben's vacant eyes, his ashen complexion, had the same tell-tale tinge of ebbing mortality.

Her throat dry, Carla told Rosa to ring for an ambulance and then fetch Mr Fitzgerald. She crouched by the bed and held Ben's hand.

"You'll be okay," she soothed. "Relax now."

Ben's face creased in agony as another spasm of pain tore through his chest. Instinctively sure of her diagnosis, Carla wondered if he had known all along what the real trouble was.

Minutes later, Jack appeared. "Have you sent for a doctor?" he asked immediately.

"Ambulance," said Carla, adding in a whisper so that

Ben could not hear, "He's in a bad way. Has he had heart trouble before?"

"Heart trouble? He's only forty-two!" Jack protested, his eyes full of concern.

"And overworked half to death," said Carla bitterly as two men arrived with a stretcher and carted Ben off.

Jack insisted on riding to the hospital in the ambulance with Ben, and asked Carla to come with them as he didn't speak Italian. It was strange to see the almost feminine tenderness he showed, holding Ben's hand between both of his and telling him not to worry, he would be just fine. Clearly Jack was badly shaken, probably out of a sense of guilt, Carla thought. She would not have expected much sentiment from a man whose success betokened hard-headed ruthlessness.

After arriving at the hospital, his gentleness was superceded by impatience and frustration as they waited interminably for news of Ben's condition. He paced the waiting room floor, completely unrecognisable from his usual cool, relaxed self. He seemed oblivious of Carla's presence, banging the fist of one hand against the palm of the other and muttering under his breath. He appeared to be blaming himself in some way for what had happened, as well he might, she reflected.

"I should have realised," he kept saying. "When he sent for me I should have known he was in trouble. I should have probed more. He's so damn secretive, so paranoid, I should have wrung it out of him. Why didn't he tell me how ill he was?"

"Because he's terrified of failure, of letting you down," Carla could not resist replying. "Goal-oriented, I think you called it."

"Don't be a sarcastic bitch," he snarled. "Show some respect. The guy could be dying in there!"

Carla shut up, swallowing the words of reproach that hovered on her lips. She felt full of disgust at what pressure did to people, full of revulsion for selling, business, the need to make money, ready to reject all the things Jack Fitzgerald stood for despite the knowledge that she herself fed well at his table. To heap stress on an individual was to administer slow poison. Broodingly, she thought back to the dark days of Pappa's sudden, short illness and premature death. If she had been guilty then, surely Jack must deserve some share of the guilt now. Sitting silently on the hospital bench while Jack paced to and fro, memories flayed her pitilessly. Forced to relive the worst period of her life, she could not check the tears which welled into her eyes and rolled down her cheeks despite her efforts to blink them back. Embarrassed, she groped in her bag for a tissue.

Jolted out of his own reverie by her distress, Jack silently handed her a handkerchief. Mortified, he put his arm around her.

"Don't cry, honey. I'm sorry if I bit your head off just then. I guess I feel responsible for what happened and I took it out on you because you happened to be around. Ben's one in a million, but he wouldn't want you crying over him. He's not family, you don't even know him that well. Save your tears for your own troubles."

Carla gulped back a sob. "My father died this way," she found herself confessing. "It's brought it all back to me, that's all."

"In that case," replied Jack softly, after a pause, "cry all you want to."

And to her dismay, she did just that. Tears she had never shed at the time or since, tears she had swallowed, had let eat into her like acid, suddenly gushed out of her uncontrollably, relentlessly, violently. He held her close, one hand behind her head, heedless of the large damp patch spreading over his teeshirt as her weeping reached torrential proportions. To cry so unexpectedly, so unashamedly, so luxuriously, left Carla feeling giddy and weak. When at last the flood abated, a white-coated doctor approached them and said in Italian that there was no need for tears, the patient would survive. There had been relatively minor damage to the heart, and as long as Ben stopped smoking and changed his life-style, he would, after three months or so, be fit again.

Jack's face was a study of relief. He plied the doctor, via Carla, with insistent questions, was assured that visitors would be allowed next day, that Ben would be moved to a private room, and that all bills would be forwarded to Jack direct.

To this end various documents had to be signed at the hospital's office, Carla busily translating, before they rode back to the complex by taxi.

"How long," mused Jack, voicing his thoughts aloud, "can this outfit carry on without Ben?"

"Are you asking me?" said Carla.

"Yes. You've been here three weeks. I've been here two days. I'd appreciate your opinion."

"How long does a kindergarten behave itself without a teacher?" replied Carla bluntly. "A sales team like this one isn't very different, all pushing and jostling and everyone out for themselves, me included. You'll have to replace him with someone tough pretty soon or there'll be anarchy."

Jack's lips twitched. This girl certainly knew the score.

"Think I'm tough enough?" he asked blandly.

"You?"

"Me. Ben will fret himself into another heart attack if he's replaced by one of his rivals – he's only just been promoted – and no-one else knows the set-up here. I guess that's what's been preying on his mind. No, I'm the only babysitter he can trust. So I'm staying."

He smiled dazzlingly. "Which means I might just have time for that crossword after all."

Ben had been doing a good job, but he had been ill. Jack Fitzgerald, bursting with health and vigour, took over with a bang. His presence acted like a strong stimulant. Carla could only marvel at the extraordinarily subtle way he galvanised people into giving their best. In no time flat, he knew everybody's name, down to the postman and the bread delivery boy. He managed to motivate Ian McIntyre into a softer, cleaner, more successful sell, began picking up basic Italian with the artless facility of a small child, and still contrived, by telephone, to keep abreast of numerous other interests on both sides of the Atlantic.

He was capable of strenuous mental athletics without showing any signs of fatigue. He remained unflappable but implacable, good-humoured but firm. Even the most hard-bitten of the sales team thought him a 'great guy' while remaining slightly in awe of him. He had the business equivalent of star quality.

Every evening, religiously, he visited Ben in hospital, taking Carla with him to interrogate the doctors. Ben had had a bad fright, and once reassured that Jack himself would be taking over, needed surprisingly little persuasion to accept the plans that had been made for him – a month at a luxurious convalescent home, and then two months' holiday, wherever he liked, all at Jack's expense.

"A cruise," Jack suggested mischievously. "Ideal for picking up a rich widow, Ben. Gentle exercise is what you need."

Resigned to abandoning Catalina to Jack's safe hands, Ben made good progress and was soon chafing to be out of hospital. Carla was uncomfortably aware now that the medical bulletins had become repetitive, and given that Jack's Italian was not quite as inadequate as he had claimed, her presence at the nightly visit was becoming superfluous. She tried to broach the subject tactfully.

"You don't need me this evening," she told him when he came to collect her as usual. "We're not expecting any news, and perhaps someone else in the team would like to go with you."

"They've all been, in their time off," he countered. "Ben will be expecting you, he'll be upset if you don't come. Besides," he added, "so will I. Now that I've learned the ropes around here, I feel I've earned some relaxation. How about going out to eat somewhere afterwards, instead of dining back here?"

"Out to eat?" she repeated flustered. "Oh, I don't think so. I mean, I'm not all that hungry. I had a huge lasagne at lunchtime. I have to watch my weight."

This careless remark invited long and careful scrutiny as Jack scanned her figure with mock concern.

"Oh, I don't know." He smiled suggestively. "You seem to put it on in all the right places so an extra pound or two won't matter. Anyway, you deserve a treat after your triumph today with the penthouse."

Jack, at the drop of a hat, knew exactly what, when and to whom they had all sold, and his unfailingly accurate acknowledgement of individual success was a great morale booster. While Ben measured sales by the units blocked out on the chart, abbreviated indicators of productivity, Jack would say, "Two weeks of 235 in August to those Germans wasn't half bad, Ian" or Steve or Carla or whoever it happened to be.

She blushed, half pleased to be congratulated, half embarrassed at the frank look of appraisal still in his eyes. But, like everyone else, she ended up doing what Jack wanted, and accepted the invitation.

Since the disastrous night of the ashtray, Carla had been studiously avoiding Ian McIntyre, but not quite as studiously as he avoided her. Carla, strongly work-

74

motivated and rather anti-social, remained blissfully unaware that her reputation as a 'wildcat' had spread throughout the team, together with a certain amount of lewd speculation regarding her relationship with Jack. Consensus of opinion was that if anyone could tame her, Jack was the man. She would meet her match, but then so would he. Carla would have been mortified had she known all this. Like most women, she vastly underrated the male capacity for gossip.

Some innate survival instinct prompted her to play down the glamour that evening. She dressed demurely in a high-necked, loose-fitting cotton dress, wore a minimum of make-up, and coiled her luxuriant hair into a rather severe chignon. Unfortunately, she still looked ravishing, and this understatement of her looks gave her an air of provocative innocence that was no protection at all.

She wished almost as soon as they drove out of the hospital car park that she had feigned a headache and stayed at home. Jack was not the type to play Dutch uncle, and by accepting this dinner date, she feared that she had unwittingly invited him to continue their still unfinished business.

She was reassured, however, as the evening progressed, to the extent of letting down her guard to a quite untypical degree. Carla habitually had all her wits about her where men were concerned. Admittedly, she had failed to pre-empt Jack's sudden kiss, and had nearly got herself raped by Ian, but those were freak situations. Although she relaxed, she was determined to be totally straight with Jack. You didn't play games with a man like that. You either went to bed with him or left well alone.

Jack, for his part, was on his very best behaviour, or so he made it appear. He wanted to know all about Carla's career to date, skilfully drawing her out without appearing to pry. In fact, he turned out to know a great deal about the theatre, something of a surprise to Carla who had assumed that his business preoccupations would leave him no time for culture. She commented on his extensive inside knowledge.

"I hate to disillusion you," he said dryly, "but my interest isn't purely artistic. I back the odd show, so I have to keep my ear to the ground."

He named a couple of recent box-office hits. Carla was disappointed.

"Why invest in productions like those? They can find backing with no trouble at all. Lots of fringe stuff never gets a chance because people are scared to put their money where their mouth is. Wouldn't you find it a lot more satisfying to give a new playwright a fighting chance?"

Jack smiled tolerantly at this rather sanctimonious outburst.

"I'm a businessman, not a philanthropist. If I feel like supporting a lost cause, there are plenty of neglected charities in need of funds. I have no interest in playing God, or in patronising dubious talent. If a guy wants to write a play, he can't expect mollycoddling. If he's really talented, he'll survive the knocks and keep on writing. If he isn't, then he's no loss. Why should I take his risks for him?"

Carla gave him a sceptical look.

"Rumour has it," she commented, quoting Ben, "that risks are something of a hobby with you."

"It may look that way, but I tend to gamble with loaded dice. That way I stand a better chance of winning." Clearly he was amused at her mixture of curiosity and disapproval. "You mustn't believe everything people say about me."

"Just who do you think says what about you? As a matter of fact, you're generally considered to be a bit

76

of a mystery."

That wasn't quite honest of her. A certain amount of enigma surrounded Jack, certainly, but there was also any amount of well-documented tittle-tattle, especially as far as his love life was concerned. His ever-changing liaisons with jet-setting females kept the gossip-columnists hard at work. Even Carla, in her ivory tower, had overheard some of the scandal.

Besides, you only had to look at him to understand why women found him attractive. Carla, considering herself immune, had given the matter some dispassionate thought and had concluded that he would have had to have been a saint, which he clearly wasn't, not to be a little bit conceited about his startling combination of looks, intelligence and charm. She struggled to reconcile her liking for Jack with a cynical mistrust of him sexually.

Good-looking egomaniacs abounded in the acting world, and Carla had been pursued by enough handsome Thespians to have become a trifle world-weary regarding masculine beauty. Oh, he was a real Hollywood specimen all right, tall, tanned, blond, blue-eyed – he should be safely locked up in celluloid not allowed to prowl around on the loose. And he was clever with it, a born manipulator, used to getting his own way. It was lucky for her, he wasn't her type. Not that Carla really knew what her type was, given her deep-rooted prejudices about men. But she had a healthy suspicion that Jack might, misguidedly, think that she was *his* type. Resolutely, she was careful not to give him the slightest, most involuntary sign of encouragement. She didn't want another fiasco on her hands.

Meanwhile, Jack's razor-sharp brain was busily trying to puzzle Carla out. He figured that she was probably bored by the usual male routine. Compliments, red roses and candlelit dinners were all, no doubt, a big yawn for her. So self-contained, so lacking in flirtatiousness, so cool on the one hand and so outrageously provocative on the other. Not that the poor girl could help the way she looked. Huge dark eyes, fantastic glossy hair, incredible legs and sinfully tempting breasts. Could it possibly be, he wondered, that she was still a virgin? No, he decided, impossible. Not at her age, not with those looks. She certainly wasn't married or divorced, he knew that from her personnel file.

He ruled out loyalty to a boyfriend back home. She had never mentioned one, and if any guy was mad enough to let her out of his sight for a whole summer, then he didn't deserve her. So while Carla chatted away about the stage, and Jack made all the right noises, his mind was otherwise occupied, clinically contemplating exactly what he would do to her when he finally got her into bed. When, not if. And soon. But perhaps not yet. Yes, that would surprise her. She was surely expecting him to make another pass at her, given his previous reckless behaviour. Keep her guessing for a bit longer. No point in risking another slapping, or a blow on the head with a heavy object. That was for dumbos like McIntyre.

Carla was indeed quite surprised when Jack took her home without so much as a good night kiss. When he innocently asked her if she would accompany him next day to a neighbouring resort and translate for him, she found herself agreeing without demur. She went to bed thinking that perhaps he had got the message after all.

In fact, it was a treat to have a day off selling, her first since she had arrived. She could well afford this indulgence as the level of her sales had remained consistent. It was a pity she couldn't send home any money till her commission was processed at the end of the contract, but she would have such a sizeable sum by then that

Mamma would soon forget the lean summer months, and at least Gabby was earning at the moment.

The next morning, Franco packed them a picnic lunch. They would eat it on the beach, Jack said, and suggested that she should wear a bikini under her sundress. A natural enough proposal, Carla told herself, fighting a ridiculous fear of revealing quite so much of herself in front of Jack. Beaches at this time of the year were always crowded, and therefore quite safe.

Jack explained to her in the car that he was thinking of buying himself a house, hence this expedition.

"I've got to like this part of the world," he said, "but it would be a busman's holiday, keeping on one of the apartments. I was thinking of somewhere more remote."

"I expect you own houses all over the place," she commented dryly, thinking ruefully of how long it took to save money, envying Jack's ability to buy a house in the way that she might buy a pint of milk.

"Wrong. I'm a natural vagrant. I live mostly in hotels."

"Why?"

"Why not? I like to move around. It seems pointless having houses standing empty and gathering dust."

"Why buy one here then? You surely won't be spending much time in it. Why not start off in New York, or London?"

"Let's just say I have a sudden hankering to have somewhere I can disappear to from time to time. Not so much a home, more of a bolt-hole. It's a sort of experiment, if you like. If it doesn't work out, no sweat. I can always sell later at a profit."

"Do you think about money all the time?" For some reason, she felt an urge to needle him. Infuriatingly, he seemed to enjoy it.

"No, not all the time. Only when I'm not thinking

about food or sex. That applies to just about the entire human race, actually. Except you, of course. I know you set your mind on higher things."

"Oh, very sarcastic."

"You asked me if I thought about money all the time. You were trying to score some kind of point, so I retaliated."

She surprised him by taking this counter-thrust in good part.

"I know I sounded pretentious when I was talking about the theatre last night," she admitted. "Sorry if I was a pain. Actually, I'm pretty preoccupied with money myself, or I'd hardly have taken this job. And, like all Italians, I adore food."

"And?"

"And what?"

"And what about sex?"

Carla had well and truly asked for that one. She shrugged and was silent.

"Are you a virgin?" asked Jack bluntly, without taking his eyes from the road.

"What a question!"

"It's an honest one. If you are, it would explain one or two things. If you're not, it raises a few interesting questions."

"Don't be ridiculous," she snapped, flustered. "At my age it's hardly likely, is it? I'm twenty-three, for goodness' sake."

"Mmm. That's what I figured," said Jack cryptically. "Don't look so pained. I'm not one either, if that makes you feel any better. At least we've discovered something in common. Here we are."

He drew up the car outside an estate agent's office and parked nonchalantly, heedless of local restrictions.

"You do the talking," he said, handing her some printed property details. "Get the keys and ask how we get there. We can find out more later if the place looks interesting."

Carla did as requested, quite bowled over by the description of the villa in question. It had eight rooms, a tennis court, swimming pool, jacuzzi, large gardens, and a private beach. The estate agent was duly obsequious, assuming that they were a married couple, taking in Carla's beauty and Jack's indefinable air of wealth and deciding that they looked a likely prospect.

"He's saying that he'll take us there, show us round, and bring us back," explained Carla, translating.

"Tell him no thanks, we prefer to go alone," responded Jack, hands in pockets, anxious to avoid a long-winded sales pitch.

By the time they reached the villa, whose remote location was reflected in its exclusive price tag, it was nearly lunch time and the midday sun was blazing down relentlessly.

"Let's have a swim," said Jack as he got out of the car. "I'm hot."

"There's no water in the pool," observed Carla.

"In the sea, stupid. Then we can have our lunch on the patio. Save getting sand in the food."

"Don't you want to look round first?"

"What's the hurry? It won't go away," said Jack, collecting towels and the car rug from the boot and descending the steps down to the secluded strip of beach. This wasn't quite what Carla had bargained for. She followed him uneasily.

"I'm not much good at swimming, actually," she prevaricated, sitting down on a towel. Jack was already kicking off his shoes.

"No problem. You won't drown with me around."

He lay down to undress, she noticed, instead of standing as most people did. Fascinated, she watched him ease himself out of his jeans in two long, sensuous, stretching movements, and arch his back to remove his sweatshirt. He seemed much bigger without his clothes, and was in splendid physical condition with not an ounce of flab, hard, muscled, nut-brown flesh glistening with fair hair. She realised that she was staring and looked hurriedly away.

"What's the matter?" he asked, leaning back on his elbows as she made no move to undress. "Aha. I get it. You think that as soon as you take your clothes off I'll start twitching and foaming at the mouth." Clearly he found her shyness vastly entertaining.

"What nonsense," bristled Carla, stepping out of her sundress without further ado.

"Wow," continued Jack, teasing. "Perhaps you were right at that."

He made a playful lunge that sent her scampering, shrieking, towards the water where, he discovered, she swam like a fish. What exactly was she afraid of? he asked himself yet again. Surely she realised he wasn't a brute?

But she finally relaxed, child-like, in the warm sea, splashing about in a quite uninhibited fashion, riding the waves, her head bobbing wetly above the water as she swam delightedly to and fro. Carla had had no leisure for weeks, and she hadn't swum in the sea for years, although she had taught her sisters to swim at the dreary municipal baths. She surrendered herself briefly to the freedom and exhilaration of this unaccustomed treat. Wisely, Jack let her enjoy herself and kept his distance, swimming lazily some distance from the shore and watching her unobserved. If only she would let go like that on dry land, he thought, they could have quite a party.

It was a long time since Jack had strategised. By nature a fast worker, he had always found females fairly predictable creatures and had never wasted time on long

82

drawn-out preliminaries. Women, in his experience, were invariably quick to get the message and respond accordingly. By his own lights, he always played fair. He never pretended love or permanence, not even with long-standing partners like Helen. He never got girls into trouble, he never set out to break hearts. He offered pleasure, and accepted it in return. Simple. Not since High School had Jack stalked his prey or used delaying tactics. Not until Carla de Luca. She had a fiery temperament which, to him, suggested latent passion. The bump on McIntyre's head proved that. Had she had an unhappy love affair, perhaps? Was she temporarily off men? Now, that had to be a challenge. Never in Jack's career had a woman turned him down.

Carla ran back up the beach ahead of him and was all wrapped up in a towel by the time he joined her. He lay down full length to dry off in the sun. Carla was already busy dabbing on sun cream. He didn't offer to help her, as she had half-expected. Instead, he waited until she had finished and then said, "Would you mind if I had some of that? You know what delicate skin we blonds have."

She handed him the tube, looking disbelievingly at his deep, year-round tan.

"You don't look likely to burn to me," she commented.

"It's just my back, actually," he explained plaintively. "It's unbelievably sensitive. Hard to reach, though. Will you rub it on for me please?" He smiled innocently.

She could hardly refuse. Kneeling over him, she began tentatively applying the cream to his smooth, hard flesh, her manner brisk and matter-of-fact as she strove to hide her acute discomfiture at being forced to touch him in this way, trying to ignore the odd tingling sensation in her fingertips. Sensing her embarrassment, Jack began teasing her unmercifully, purring like a pantomime cat and emitting exaggerated "oohs" and "aahs" until, despite herself, she was giggling helplessly.

"It's all very well for you to laugh, you hussy," he complained. "I can't roll back over again now without disgracing myself, and it's all your fault. Obviously you enjoy tormenting poor trusting men. I asked you to rub in a little bit of sun cream, not give me a Swedish massage. I'll get my own back on you later. Now take your wicked wanton self back to the car and fix me some lunch. I might just be decent by the time it's ready."

Despite the outrageousness of this speech, Carla was quite disarmed. A sense of humour was not Remo's strong point, neither was it most men's when it came to sex. She could only hope that Jack's sense of the ridiculous would stand him in good stead when he finally realised that there was nothing doing. He was working up to something, she had been naive to think he wouldn't. It was a pity he had to spoil things when she enjoyed his company so much. But she found that she was no longer actually afraid of Jack. Just afraid, as always, of herself.

Before long, cold chicken, salami, olives, tomatoes, bread, fruit and wine were laid out temptingly on one of the patio tables. Munching on a stick of celery, Carla surveyed the villa from the outside. Although recently built, it observed the local architectural traditions, and had obviously been individually designed for somebody very rich. Through the windows she could see the expensive decor and marble floors, showing that no expense had been spared, not that it should have been, judging by the price. She strolled through the gardens, admiring the well kept shrubbery and lawns, returning to find Jack, mercifully dressed again, pouring out the wine.

"*Salute*," he said, and began eating. Carla was very hungry after her swim, and together they set about demolishing their picnic.

"Did you enjoy that?" asked Jack at length, leaning back in his chair and sipping hot coffee she had poured him from a flask.

"It was delicious. I told you, I'm terribly greedy. At home I force myself to live on salad and yoghurt, except for when I visit my mother or help out at the Isola Bella. If I didn't starve myself periodically, I'd be enormous."

"The Isola Bella? That's a restaurant?"

"Yes. I live above it, in Soho. The owners are sort of relations, and I do a bit of waitressing for them when I'm out of work. Good tips, no tax, and all the pasta I can eat. Which is quite a lot."

Jack smiled. "Eat all you want, sweetheart. But watch how much wine you drink." He refilled her glass. "Remember what happens when you get smashed."

"Must you keep referring to that unfortunate incident?" she grumbled. "I don't know which was worse, nearly killing Ian or being sick all over you. I can assure you, I learned my lesson."

Jack looked at her levelly, then put down his coffee and said unexpectedly, "Carla, is there something I ought to know about you? Some deep dark secret in your past?"

"I really don't know what you mean. What on earth has my past to do with you? Shall we look round the house now?"

"Don't change the subject. I just want to know why you're so buttoned up. Why you're so wary of men in general and me in particular. What happened?"

"Nothing 'happened'! Really, Jack, just because I don't throw myself at you doesn't mean I'm warped, you know. You can't expect every woman to fall into bed with you."

"I don't. Just the ones I want to fall into bed with. You, for example, as you very well know. Don't worry, I got all your little messages to keep off, but if you don't give me some kind of reason, I might start taking it personally and develop all kinds of complexes."

"Please, Jack, leave it alone. I don't have to give you a reason, and you've no need to take anything personally. If you want reassurance that you're attractive, there are plenty of other women who will be glad to restore your self-esteem. It's absolutely nothing to do with you. I'm just not interested – not with you or with anyone else right now, thank you very much. Okay?" Her voice trembled. She didn't want to discuss this, not with Jack.

"What did he do to you, Carla?" Jack continued undeterred. "Rape you? Beat you up? Jilt you?"

"No-one did anything to me. I told you, I'm just not interested. We can't all have your preoccupation with sex."

"I'm too busy being occupied to be preoccupied," pointed out Jack mildly. "You're the one who's preoccupied."

"Stop trying to psychoanalyse me. My sex life is none of your business."

"Yes it is. Or rather, it soon will be. Carla, I'd hate to upset you, or frighten you, or rake up bad memories. If I understand what the problem is, then we stand more of a chance together."

"You are unbelievably arrogant. I have absolutely no intention of going to bed with you."

"Don't swim against the current, Carla. You're on some kind of hunger strike, and I won't know why unless you tell me. I don't aim to force-feed you. I just want you to get your appetite back, before you starve to death."

Carla exploded.

"For goodness' sake! You may be my employer, but that gives you absolutely *no right* to interfere in my private life. You just cannot believe, can you, that any woman could turn you down? You really do think that you're irresistible. Well, you're not. What you *are* is conceited, misguided, and worst of all incapable of taking a hint. You have a one track mind. You brought me here today with one aim, and because I don't want to know you try to make me feel like some kind of freak! Well, okay, if it saves your pride, I *am* a freak. *I don't like sex!* Got it? Happy now?"

Jack took the barrage of insults calmly, looking at her unwaveringly. She had, as he had intended, lost her cool. She was wild-eyed, flushed, beside herself with fury. Out of the blue, he felt a curious shaft of insight.

"Was it an abortion?" he asked gently, regretting the question almost immediately. Carla's face went white. Without another word she got up from the table, turned on her heel and fled.

Appalled at her reaction, Jack sat silent and motionless as she ran off into the gardens like a scalded cat. Wisely, he let her be for a while, packing up the picnic things, reloading the car, and wishing too late that he'd handled her more cautiously. She had a low flashpoint all right. Highly inflammable, handle with care. Had he hit the nail on the head, or simply offended her beyond endurance? Poor kid, he lectured himself, why can't you just leave her be? Quit hounding her, admit defeat. What the hell was he trying to prove anyhow?

Sighing, he went to seek her out and make his apologies. She was sitting, dry-eyed, on the back steps, staring vacantly ahead of her. Unaware of his approach, unobserved, she looked small, lost, pathetic. Jack, never a sentimentalist, felt an unfamiliar pang of conscience and decided he didn't like it. This whole thing was getting over-emotional, out of hand. Sex was fun, not a drama. Why waste energy on a lame duck? God, she was beautiful.

Crossing over to where she sat, he stood silently until

she looked up. She was no longer angry. Her face was calm, contrite almost.

"I'm sorry about the performance just now," she said coolly. "I went over the top. Occupational hazard. I know you meant well, but if you walk through a minefield you have to expect the odd explosion."

Boldly, Carla forced herself to look him straight in the eye, her expression defiant yet pleading. He was so strong, she thought, so solid. So straightforward and direct. So relaxed and funny. And now everything was going to get messy, and complicated, and unmanageable.

"I really like you, Jack," she said, amazed at her own candour. "Please let me feel I can trust you as well."

"Trust me? To do what?"

"Not to."

"Then you can't trust me," he replied flatly, with just the hint of a wry smile. "But at least you know I won't lie about it."

Surprisingly, that was good enough. Carla held out her hand. He took it, entwining her fingers in his, and squeezed it. Then he bent down and tilted her chin and for one tantalising, agonising moment, she was sure he was going to kiss her. But he didn't.

"Let's go see the house," he said, and pulled her to her feet.

"No," pronounced Jack, as they went from room to room. "No, no, no."

"What's wrong with it?" protested Carla. "It's got everything!"

"That's the trouble. It's got no character, it's too perfect, too contrived, too market-researched. There's no feel to it. You might just as well stay in a hotel and be done with it.

"Every millionaire loves a baked apple," quoted

Carla. "I suppose you'd prefer to slum it with the peasants up in dem dere hills."

"That might not be a bad idea at that. Somewhere old and lived in with a bit of history. Somewhere that's seen a few births and deaths. Somewhere I can renovate and personalize. Not a gin palace like this."

Carla shrugged. "You'd simply adore my bedsitter," she remarked dryly. "Or my Mamma's house in Ealing. Pity we can't swap. You're spoiled, that's all."

Jack seemed amused. "Is that what you think? That I'm a spoiled rich kid?"

Carla pursed her lips. "Wait for it. You're about to tell me that you grew up in a tenement on the Lower East Side and fought your way to the top."

"Oh, I wish I could. That would shut you up nicely, wouldn't it?" He smiled without rancour but didn't, however, seem disposed to enlighten her further.

"Well?" she demanded eventually, her curiosity getting the better of her. "What about a bit of your murky past for a change? Fair's fair."

"My murky past, huh? Well, the first girl I ever –"

"Jack! You know perfectly well I don't mean that."

"Okay, potted biography coming up. I was raised in Queen's – that's a sort of New York equivalent of your Ealing, I guess. Third generation immigrant stock, lower middle class. Father Irish/Scandinavian, mother Polish/Austrian. I just settle for being American, it's useful shorthand. My parents both died within a few months of each other when Steve and I were teenage, so we went to stay with my mother's sister and her husband in Connecticut. They did their duty by us, but I suppose we were at a difficult age, and at the end of the day we weren't their kids. Being with them always felt like charity, somehow, and I jumped the nest as soon as I could. Steve had more sense. He went to College, did a lot of social climbing, married the boss's

89

daughter, the whole works.

"I just bummed around after I left school, one casual job after another, living from day to day. I didn't get any qualifications but I sure grew up fast. Then I got drafted and that changed my outlook a bit. Being cooped up with a load of other guys gives you a hell of a lot of time to think. I started to make plans. I decided that when I got out, I would get rich."

"And that's what you did?"

"That's what I did. The day I got out of uniform, I had a few hundred dollars between me and another dead-end job. I gambled it all on the stock exchange. I won, and gambled some more, and kept winning. That's how it all started and I've never looked back. Nothing noble, nothing sinister, nothing mysterious. Sorry to disappoint you. But I wasn't born rich, although people always assume I was. It bugs me."

"Why? Because you want credit for your success?"

"No. Because I hate being labelled."

"You'd hate being a woman, then," said Carla. "That's the biggest label of them all." She bit her lip, aware that she had just invited further psychoanalysis.

"I remember," reminisced Jack, leaning back against the wall, arms folded, "my Aunt Sophie's kitchen. Rows of those canisters, she had, with labels on – coffee, sugar, flour and so on. She had a perfect system. When she wanted rice, she went to the jar labelled currants. You see, the currants were in the jar labelled tea. And the tea..."

But Carla was already laughing.

"So, don't think a big label marked 'woman' takes .me in for a moment," he finished. "I know a tigress when I see one. Even if McIntyre didn't."

He ruffled her hair, smiling, and they set off for home.

Chapter Five

Because of Ben's illness and their joint trips to the hospital, Carla had seen Jack every evening since his arrival at Catalina. Ben, however, flew back to England the next day and for the following week she saw no more of Jack than any other member of the team. The chief reason was the unannounced arrival of Helen Fitzgerald who had come, it appeared, for a short holiday although popular rumour assumed that she wanted to keep an eye on Jack.

Jack did not seem in the least put out by Helen's inviting herself. She installed herself in his apartment as of right, and could be seen daily beside the pool working hard on her tan. She was the type of sun worshipper who needed no books or other diversions to break the monotony. Apart from rearranging her body periodically like a chicken on a spit, and applying generous bastings of sun oil, she did nothing but lie there all day and every day, supremely indolent, joining Jack in the trattoria for lunch and completely monopolising him all evening.

Helen had precisely the sort of looks Carla had always envied. Blonde, very slim, and expensively fragile, she looked every inch the 'boss's daughter'. Money and breeding oozed out of every elegant pore. She was exactly the sort of woman you'd expect Jack to have in tow, a creature of film premières and very dry Martinis.

Gossip, of course, was endemic. Infuriatingly, it would cease abruptly the moment Carla came within earshot. She became the subject of knowing, if sympathetic, glances. People hoped vaguely for a showdown, no doubt expecting that Carla and Helen would eventually have some kind of confrontation as rivals for Jack's attention. Jack himself, however, remained imperturbable. He treated Carla just like any other colleague, and Helen as if he had been married to her for years. He showed her no overt affection, did not allow her to interfere with his work, and made love to her uncomplainingly on demand. At first mildly irritated by Helen's ill-timed arrival, he had decided that he might as well exploit it, wondering if her presence might act as a catalyst on the unpredictable Carla.

She rose to the occasion with dignity. She was civil to Jack, and very civil indeed to Helen. Her output increased. She appeared absorbed in her job, and as unsociable as ever. Jack was disappointed. It seemed to suit her just fine having Helen around, to divert his unwelcome advances. Determined not to show his chagrin, Jack made the most of Helen's availability. After all, he was only human. Meanwhile, Carla did inordinate amounts of yoga.

One particuarly hot, steamy night, she was fighting a fairly hopeless battle with insomnia. Nothing to do with Jack Fitzgerald, of course, she was keeping her thoughts firmly off *that* subject. No, it was just this infernal heatwave, this stifling humidity. Seeing the hands of her watch move round to three a.m., she finally got out of bed, slipped on her bikini, and picked up a towel. A nice refreshing swim was what she needed. She would tire herself out and cool herself off at the same time.

Carla's bedroom overlooked the pool, as did all the

others in that block, but access to it involved going down in the lift to the rear exit of the building and walking round to the front again. Given the lateness of the hour, she decided to take a short cut by walking across the six adjoining balconies to the side steps which led directly down to the pool area.

The balconies were divided by low parapets, about three feet high. Quietly, Carla swung her legs over each one, landing gracefully and silently on the other side. As she swivelled herself over the boundary between 314 and 315, however, one of her flip-flop sandals slipped off and bounced into the gloom of Jack's balcony. Anxious to retrieve it, she crept back, and was groping in the dark on her hands and knees when she froze to the spot.

Amplified on the still night air through the open sliding doors came the sound of voices, Jack's and Helen's. Soft, low, intimate, their indistinct exchange of sighs and murmurs drifted tantalisingly, suggestively, mockingly, out on to the veranda. Appalled to find herself eavesdropping, and shocked at the sudden, vivid images that flooded her senses, Carla was forced finally, inescapably, to face the truth she had tried so hard to deny. That she wished it were she, and not Helen, who lay in that bed; she, and not Helen, who –

Blocking this line of thought with an effort, gripping her sandal in her hand, Carla climbed gingerly over the parapet, fairly leapt the remaining ones, fled down the steps and plunged into the cool, soothing waters of the pool. She swam abstractedly for a long time. It didn't help particularly. She remained agitated, disturbed, aroused, for reasons she steadfastly refused to admit. In her search for oblivion, she swam herself into exhaustion. When she finally heaved herself out of the water, legs like lead, and walked slowly back to her apartment, the long way round this time, she fell into bed and slept instantly, only to fall prey to violently explicit, erotic dreams.

When she reported for work next day, bleary-eyed and slightly dopey, she ran straight into Jack who was studying the sales chart while drinking black coffee. Fresh, vital and wide awake, he had evidently slept like a top. Carla's first instinct was to walk right out again. She didn't feel able to meet his eye.

"Morning, Carla," he greeted her cheerfully. "Enjoy your swim?"

"What?" faltered Carla, egg all over her face.

"Last night. I heard you splashing about. I was tempted to join you, I must admit. Terribly hot and humid, wasn't it? If I'd built this place from scratch, I'd have put in air conditioning. Opening the window is no help at all. What's the matter? Something on your mind?"

"No," mumbled Carla, confused. "I just didn't sleep well, as you know."

"You've been avoiding me all week," he observed blandly. "I hoped at first it was because you might be a bit put out. Very conceited of me. You'll be sorry to hear that Helen's flying home today for a family wedding. I've got an important meeting this morning I can't get out of so I was hoping you'd take her to the airport for me."

"Me? Why me? Why not ask one of the men?"

"What a sexist suggestion. I thought you didn't like being labelled. What's the problem? She won't scratch your eyes out, you know, she's got no idea I lust after you. And even if she did, insecurity isn't one of her vices."

Carla, devoid of repartee, could think of nothing to say.

"It's the 12.30 flight to Rome," Jack continued. "I told her you'd pick her up at ten so she'd be ready by half-past. Take the Alfasud."

He pulled the car keys out of his pocket and handed them to her. It was already too late for protests as other team members came in and demanded his attention.

Furious, Carla's only resort was not to show her annoyance. Jack would be bound, in his egotistical fashion, to interpret her reluctance the wrong way. Ill-humouredly, she went to tell the resident odd-job man to collect Mrs Fitzgerald's luggage at the appointed time and load it into the car. There was no point in starting any work this morning so she spent a sullen hour painting her nails a predatory scarlet. She changed back into casual clothes, and tied a bandanna, Apache-style, around her head, a couldn't-care-less style of garb that would give the lie to any suggestion of competitiveness. Then she sat in the car with the windows down, stubbornly admiring the view until Helen, late as usual, slipped in beside her, tanned and immaculate in a white trouser suit impregnated with neat Arpège.

Jack had introduced Helen to all the team, but beyond the usual social courtesies, the two women were barely acquainted. Helen, however, knew all she needed to know about Carla, and had never kidded herself for a moment. The Jack she knew and loved so well would never be able to leave this girl alone. She smiled cordially.

"Nice of you to take time out to give me a lift," she cooed. "These local cab drivers scare the hell out of me."

"No trouble," muttered Carla, putting the car into gear and screeching out of the driveway with rather too many revs.

"Jack's told me so much about you," continued Helen innocently. Carla remained poker-faced. "I was with him that day he spotted you in London. Would you believe, I bought six of those Wonderblouse things. The

95

odd thing was, they just didn't look the same when I tried them on at home. Guess Jack was right. He said you were a smart cookie."

Carla, despite herself, thawed slightly. Helen, with her casual drawl spattered with American idioms, was oddly disarming.

"I understand that you're an actress," she continued. Carla squirmed imperceptibly in her seat. She didn't like the thought of Jack discussing her with this woman. What exactly had he said about her? she wondered.

"That's right. Out of work, I'm afraid. As usual."

"Same story back home. What you might call an over-crowded profession, huh? Jack's crazy about the theatre, of course. I guess he's told you that."

"We – er – don't have the same tastes, actually," said Carla rather loftily.

"You don't say? I sympathise. All that highbrow, wayout stuff leaves me cold, too. Off-Broadway, that's Jack's style. Give me a show with a few laughs and comfortable seats."

Helen prattled on while Carla analysed this unexpected information. So he wasn't a confirmed lowbrow after all. He actually preferred experimental drama, despite his refusal to invest in it and his cynical disregard for struggling playwrights. He went to watch real theatre and let it die prematurely while he put his money into sure-fire hits. In much the same way as he admired Carla while putting his money on Helen. Well, he'd admitted he gambled with loaded dice.

A silence fell, thanks to Carla's abstracted lack of response.

"Say," remarked Helen, noticing her faraway look, "something bugging you?"

"What? No, no, of course not. I was miles away. Sorry. What were you saying?"

"Nothing. Is it Jack?"

"Pardon?"

"Is that what's bugging you? Is it Jack?"

"Why should Jack be, er . . . bugging me?"

"Honey, I wasn't born yesterday. You're the only woman on the team and I know Jack inside out. Did I break up the party?"

Carla tried hard to concentrate on her driving.

"I'm afraid I don't know what you mean," she said levelly.

"Do me a favour, honey. I've seen it all before, remember? Sooner or later, I tell myself, age will catch up with Jack and he'll give in and settle down. I'm not proud. My private life's an open book, you should read the scandal sheets back home. I'm keeping a scrap book for when I'm old and grey. Have all the fun you want, Carla, but don't forget he always comes back to me in the end, boomerang-style, know what I mean? Don't go breaking your heart over him. You look kinda jumpy to me. Take it easy. Play it for laughs. No hard feelings, huh? We girls ought to understand each other."

Carla was flabbergasted to the point of speechlessness.

"Mrs Fitzgerald, I can assure you . . ."

"Sorry, honey, I've embarrassed you. What Jack would call my big mouth. Relax. Have fun. Just don't get in too deep. You're a nice kid and Jack . . . well, figuratively speaking, he doesn't know his own strength. So be careful. Love is something he can't understand. Apart from the physical kind, that is. He sure knows all about that."

Poor Carla was by now blushing scarlet, to Helen's obvious amusement. Shrugging, she lit a king-size cigarette, squeezed Carla's arm in sisterly fashion, and kindly let the subject drop.

Carla didn't bother to let Jack know Helen had got off

all right. She drove back from Pisa at breakneck speed, locked the car, changed into a dress, accosted some elderly Swedes and sold them a month of December sea-view studio in record time. Well, it would no doubt seem warm to them.

Triumphantly picking up the red magic marker to block in four squares, she went to help herself to Coke from the dispenser.

"So you're back," came Jack's voice behind her. "Flight take off on time?"

"No problem," she confirmed, without turning round. She took a long cool swallow.

"I didn't see you at lunch," Jack continued mildly.

"I didn't have any. I wasn't hungry."

"Come out to dinner tonight to make up for it."

"No thanks."

"Why not?"

"I'm busy."

"Doing what? Skulking in your room till it's time for a midnight swim?"

Carla coloured.

"Why don't you leave me alone?" she snapped, turning round. "And anyway, what about Helen?"

"What about Helen?"

"For goodness' sake, as soon as her back's turned, you—"

"You've misread the situation, honey."

"On the contrary, I read the situation loud and clear. Helen's gone home, so you've started sniffing round me again."

"Jealous?"

"I was waiting for that. Of course I'm not."

"Jealousy's dumb. Helen doesn't suffer from it, I can assure you. Neither do I, which is just as well. You don't suppose she's going back to a nunnery, do you?"

"You — you disgust me!"

"I guess that's a good sign. Better than total indifference, anyhow. I'll pick you up around eight."

The telephone rang, and he was soon immersed in other things.

It was impossible, of course, to escape. The complex was like a goldfish bowl, there was nowhere for her to hide. Determined not to be beaten, she changed after work into old jeans and a suntop, and washed her hair so that when Jack called for her, looking cool in a cream safari suit, she had a towel round her head and looked, as far as she was able, a mess.

"I've got a headache," she pouted. "I can't come out tonight."

"You certainly can't, looking like that," he agreed. Without another word he turned on his heel and departed.

Well, that was what she had wanted, wasn't it? Carla thought petulantly, as hunger pangs began to gnaw at her. She hadn't, she realised, eaten a thing all day. She dried her hair ill-temperedly, bit ravenously into an apple, switched on the television and resigned herself to watching an ancient western with Italian sub-titles. Amid the frenzied banging and shooting, and the crunching noises of her apple, she didn't, at first, hear the knock at her door. It was Franco, beaming atop a loaded tray.

"Sorry to hear you got a headache, Carla," he sympathised, setting down his burden on the dining table, a junior waiter following with a bottle of Chianti, bread, and iced water. "*Buon appetito*," they chorused, tactfully making themselves scarce as Jack appeared in the doorway, thanking them and wishing them goodnight. Without speaking, he switched off the television and began pouring the wine.

"All your favourites," he announced dryly. "Antipasti. *Risotto Milanese*. Pistachio ice cream. We'd better put that in the ice box. Nice and digestible for an invalid, I thought," he added mischievously, pulling out the chairs.

Carla, her thick, heavy hair all over the place, her cheeks flushed and her nose shiny from the dryer, gaped helplessly at the table. Jack solemnly popped an olive into her open mouth. Catching the twinkle in his eye, her lips twitched first into a rueful smile then into a defeated laugh.

"You never give up, do you?" she asked.

"You ain't seen nothing yet, lady. Sit down. I'm hungry, even if you're not."

It was impossible to remain formal as they piled their plates with tempting hors-d'oeuvres and helped each other to the crusty bread, especially as Jack insisted on conducting the conversation in his rapidly improving but still very limited Italian, with all the unselfconsciousness of the born linguist. He was an extraordinarily difficult man to hold back from, thought Carla. He created an atmosphere of intimacy out of thin air. Soon his literal translations of English idioms had her rocking with laughter.

"Don't mock, it's not polite," Jack reproached her finally. "It's all very well for you to laugh, you never had to learn. It puts me at a great disadvantage, out here, needing a translator or relying on people to speak English. What I need is practice. Perhaps you could start giving me a few lessons."

"Is that just an excuse?"

"For what?"

"For spending time with me," she elaborated, wishing she hadn't spoken.

"You think I need an excuse for that? You're over-reacting, as usual. If you weren't around, I guess I'd have to ask somebody else. Books and tapes are okay but they only give you a base. Luckily, I learn fast and speak quite good Spanish, which helps. Mexican Spanish, admittedly, but I get by."

Carla shrugged. "If you insist. But I'm not much good at the grammar or the written side. We speak it at home, that's all. And apparently I've got a shocking Neopolitan accent, not that I've ever visited Naples." Nor ever would, she reflected. Not if she could help it . . .

"Forget about the grammar. I learn like a parrot. Very unscientific. You know, my mother grew up speaking Polish and German, but she never passed them on to my brother or me. Pop wouldn't have understood either language, so I guess that's why she didn't bother. Pity, really, kids learn so easily."

"That can be a problem, actually. After Pappa died – he always made us speak English on Sundays and at mealtimes – it turned out that Francesca just wasn't picking up any English. Mamma was very lax about it, and it slowed her down when she first started school".

"Francesca?"

"She's the youngest," explained Carla, pointing with her fork at the family photograph on the coffee table. Jack picked it up and scrutinised it.

"What a beautiful child," he said. "Did you look like that when you were her age?"

"No, I was always an ugly duckling. Braces on my teeth and lots of puppy fat. Francesca's always been the beauty of the family."

"And you all spoil her."

"Inevitably. But, luckily, she's got a very sweet nature. For example . . ."

Jack listened, fascinated, as Carla, animated now, dropped her guard to recount various amusing anecdotes on the subject. She had, it was clear, a lot of strong family feeling beneath that self-sufficient exterior.

"I guess it must be nice to come from a big family,"

mused Jack. "Now Steve's dead – he crashed his private plane a couple of years back – I'm the only Fitzgerald left. Still, perhaps that's just as well. You like kids, I take it."

"Uh-huh," said Carla, her mouth full. "It's just a shame they have to grow up. Take my sister Angela, she's at a really awkward age . . ."

"Don't you want children of your own one day?"

Carla swallowed, and gave her characteristic evasive shrug.

"I suppose so," she mumbled, non-committally.

"Going to have them by artificial insemination?"

"Don't be ridiculous. Can I have some more water please?"

"Seriously," went on Jack stubbornly, pouring some as requested, "it's all the rage in the States. Single women can get themselves pregnant by donor at special clinics. Brainy guys only, I understand. Leastways, they've never approached me. Don't you have those set-ups in England yet?"

"You're trying to make fun of me."

"Not really. I was just thinking, looking at your face light up just now, what a natural mother you'd make. You should spend less time fighting your own nature and get to understand yourself better."

"We're not back on that old tack again, are we? Next thing you'll be suggesting I see your analyst."

"Don't have an analyst. Haven't got the time. Ready for your ice-cream?"

"No thanks, I can't manage another thing. I hit the antipasti too hard, as usual. Perhaps I'll feel like some later."

"Good idea." He began pouring coffee from a vacuum jug, and set out the cups next to the settee where Carla joined him at a safe distance.

"Hell, Carla, I'm not infectious," he complained.

"Come on. You can do better than that."

Chastened, she moved closer to him.

"Now pay attention," he said, "and grit your teeth, or whatever it is that you do. I'm about to put my arm around you. It's very clean and quite harmless. Okay?"

It was okay. It was comfortable, reassuring almost, replete with food and wine, and pleasantly drowsy, to lean back against his arm and rest her head on his shoulder. Having missed most of the previous night's sleep, and tired out by her drive to Pisa and back, Carla's eyelids finally gave up the struggle. Leaving her coffee untouched, she gradually slumped against her human pillow and fell fast asleep.

Jack, pinned against the corner of the couch and unable to move without waking her, nobly allowed his own coffee to get cold and resisted every temptation to take advantage of the moment, kiss her into submission, and carry her off to bed. The warm, soft weight of her body pressed against his, the smell of her newly-washed hair and the quiet, regular sound of her breathing were almost unbearably arousing. It was a totally new experience for Jack to fight his natural urges. He had never wanted to, nor needed to, let alone tried to. Jump on her now, he reminded himself, and you'll blow the whole thing.

He looked steadfastly at the ill-starred ashtray and smiled to himself as she continued, exhausted, to sleep like a baby. Occasionally she sighed and wriggled, burrowing into him uninhibitedly in her slumber. Jack felt a wave of something new, unfamiliar, disturbing. He couldn't quite define it because he had not encountered it before. But whatever it was, it must have calmed his desire because, as the hands moved round to midnight, he joined her in a deep, companionable sleep.

They were woken simultaneously by a deafening roll of thunder, followed almost immediately by a dazzling

103

flash of lightning. Carla nearly leapt out of her skin. Confused, she pressed her hands to her ears.

"Relax," Jack soothed her. "It's only a storm. Just what we need with this heatwave."

His words were lost in a second roll, even louder than the first, followed by more lightning and torrential rain which came driving in through the open window. Jack got up and shut it tightly, and then went to check those in the bedroom and bathroom.

"Batten down the hatches," he called cheerfully. "What you might call a rude awakening. More coffee?"

He looked out through the curtains as the walls vibrated again.

"I love thunder, don't you?" he continued, watching the sky light up. When Carla didn't comment, he turned round to see that she was pale and trembling.

"N-no," she admitted, and then, unthinkingly, "I'm glad you're here. I've always been t-terrified of thunder."

"No kidding?"

Carla shook her head, fighting her shame at revealing this childish phobia, repressing the urge to hide under the table like a startled cat.

"Honey, you're shaking," he said, concerned. "You need some brandy. Do you have any?"

Carla shook her head again, teeth chattering as the elements continued to do noisy battle.

"I've got some in my apartment," said Jack, reaching for his jacket. "I'll go fetch it."

"No!" she protested. "Please – don't leave me."

"You want me to stay the night?" he teased, stroking her hair, touched by her terror. She didn't answer.

"Listen, why don't you hop into bed and get some sleep? I promise I won't go till the storm's over."

"No. I'll stay in here with you, on the settee," said Carla, sitting there rigid as a board.

"You look real comfortable, I must say. Come on, be a good girl and do as you're told for a change."

Without more ado, he picked her up bodily and stood for a moment as she lay in his arms, looking deep into the dark pools of her eyes.

"I'll sit right by you on the bed and hold your hand. No monkey business, honest Injun."

Carla nodded gratefully. He carried her into the bedroom, sat her on the bed, and knelt down to take off her shoes.

"Now get undressed. I won't look."

Carla wriggled out of her jeans and top and pulled a short nightie over her head. Normally she didn't bother with one in this hot weather, but it made her feel more secure. Jack untucked the covers.

"Attagirl. In you get," he said, pulling the sheet over her and sitting down on the edge of the bed. Like all the apartment beds, it was a double. What a waste, he thought to himself. She looked so small, lying in it all on her own.

"Now go to sleep. I won't leave you."

He must be quite mad, he reflected, sitting up all night holding hands with a woman instead of – But she looked all of fourteen years old, wide-eyed and terrified as the storm unleashed itself with renewed frenzy. He patted her hand and tried to see the funny side. At least he'd had a couple of hours' sleep on the couch. And when the storm stopped, however long that took, he would creep back to his own apartment and hit the sack.

Mortified at her own cowardice, Carla lay back helplessly, clutching his strong warm hand like a talisman. She could only vaguely remember falling asleep on the settee, drugged by a sensation of warmth, security and comfort, of peace and contentment. She looked at Jack's silhouette in the dark, his fair hair reflecting the moonlight, his broad back a shield against the night-time bogeys.

"Jack," she heard her voice saying, "You'll get cold."

"I'm just fine, honey. Get some sleep now."

"You can't sit up like that all night."

"Try me."

"I'll be all right now, honestly," she protested, only to dive under the bedclothes as lightning tore through the curtains, illuminating the whole room with sinister white light.

"Sure you'll be all right," he laughed. "Okay if I go now?"

She peeped out from under the sheet, only her eyes showing. Her voice muffled beneath the covers, he distinctly heard her say. "You can share the bed, if you like."

"Sorry? I didn't catch that,"

"I said," gulped Carla, "you might as well get into bed. You'd be a lot more comfortable and at least you'd get some sleep."

Comfortable, thought Jack. She had to be kidding. As for sleep . . . Play it cool, he told himself.

"Not a bad idea." He shrugged with apparent indifference and, before she got a chance to change her mind, began undressing. Carla buried her face in the pillows as she felt the bed move under his weight.

"Good night," said Jack, reaching behind him for her hand. Resolutely, he kept his back to her. Best to be on the safe side, he thought, unable to trust the forces of nature and not wishing to inadvertently frighten the poor girl out of her wits.

"Good night," she murmured, holding on to his hand for dear life until gradually her grip slackened and fear gave way to fatigue.

That night was the most acutely erotic experience of Jack's full and adventurous life to date. Tormented by her warmth, her scent, her nearness, how he ever fell asleep himself he did not know, but he must have done so eventually because some hours later he awoke to a brand new sunny morning and Carla shyly offering him coffee. He sat up in bed and rubbed his eyes.

"What time is it?" he asked sleepily, remembering with a jolt where he was.

"Seven-thirty," she said, averting her eyes as he stretched his muscular torso like a jungle cat and ran his fingers through hair tousled from sleep, giving him an uncharacteristically boyish look. She waited while he drank his coffee.

"Thank you," she said, a trifle awkwardly, "for staying last night. I really appreciated it."

"My pleasure," he said dryly, handing her the empty cup. "Mind if I take a shower?"

"Go ahead," replied Carla, indicating the door to the bathroom. She stood fixed to the spot, looking at him with an odd, faraway expression in her eyes.

"Er ... Carla," Jack began tactfully. "Don't get me wrong. I'm not shy, but I know you are. Seeing as I didn't bring my silk pyjamas with me, I –"

Coming to with a start, Carla got the message and hurried from the room.

She had woken long before Jack as the first bright morning light had filtered through the drapes. She was aware, as she resurfaced, of a delicious sensation of heat – not the oppressive, sticky heat of two nights ago, but an all-encompassing, sensuous languor as if she were soaking in a deep, luxurious bath. Only then did she see, with something like shock, the source of this unfamiliar warmth lying beside her, and remember, disbelievingly, that he was there at her invitation.

Carefully, for fear of disturbing him, she raised herself on one elbow and looked down intently at his sleeping face. He was stretched out full length on his back, arms above his head, his posture extrovert even in sleep, the covers half-way down his bare chest. His face was heavily stubbled with overnight growth, his thick fair hair falling over his forehead. It was an unfamiliar luxury to be able to lie there and inspect him in so leisurely, so unobserved a fashion. So wary had she been of eye contact, so careful not to give anything away, that she had never looked at Jack, really looked at him, close to, as she was doing now in such illicit fashion.

It was an honest face, she decided, the lines etched by his thirty-four years signalling humour, courage and tenacity. With the vivid blue of his eyes shuttered, and his features relaxed in slumber, she had nothing to fear from the incisive, penetrating candour of his waking gaze. She looked her fill, long and hard, resisting a new and powerful impulse to touch, to feel, to taste. Had Jack had the slightest inkling of this growing awareness, these suppressed urges, he would no doubt have woken with alacrity. But, having lain thoughtful till dawn, he slept deeply, innocent that it was now Carla's turn to experience, with poetic justice, the pangs of thwarted desire.

Remembering, regretting, resisting, surrendering, Carla did battle with the buried feelings which rose up to flay her, mock her, tempt her. Her lonely bed, a solitary craft adrift on a sea of wakefulness and disturbed dreams, had found by chance safe harbour in a tranquil bay, Jack's presence an anchor against the tide and winds.

With a painful stab of insight, she suddenly realised that she was looking at the one man who could save her. But who wouldn't.

Jack deliberately avoided Carla for the next few days. Having been turned on to an almost unbearable degree, he found he simply didn't trust himself enough to submit voluntarily to further torture. He positively threw himself into his work, telephoning long-distance across four time zones until late at night. Everybody noticed the change in him, the untypical tension, the suppressed impatience, the hint of fatigue, normal enough in anyone with Jack's responsibilities except Jack himself.

The climax came when he finally lost his cool and hauled one unfortunate member of the team over the coals for what was, admittedly, a cardinal error. Phil Townsend, a born salesman but careless on paperwork, had failed to block out a sale on the master chart with the result that Carla had, in good faith, double-sold it.

Phil rather unwisely argued that his client should keep the week in question. He had made the sale first. It was tough on Carla, but it could happen to anyone. Carla, terrified by the blazing blue of Jack's eyes, was only too ready to agree with Phil. She would, she burbled, contact her clients at their hotel; she had a good chance of getting them to switch apartments or buy an alternative week.

Jack froze her with a look and overruled her coldly and logically. Phil had made the error, therefore he would lose the sale, and the commission, and the client. Useless for Phil to protest that his clients had already returned to Frankfurt, that the sale had been touch and go in the first place, and to suggest that Carla should ring her clients first to see if they could salvage both sales. Jack was implacable, leaving the forceful and argumentative Phil totally flattened.

"Whew," he commented as they left Jack's office. "When he blows his top, there's quite a bang. No hard feelings, Carla. You can't help the way he feels about you."

She was horrified.

"Phil, you don't mean that! I'm sorry you lost out, I did my best to help, but when all's said and done Jack was perfectly fair. If our positions had been reversed, *I* would have got the rocket and *you* would have kept the sale."

"Anything you say, Carla," smirked Phil with mock gallantry, in a manner that suggested, infuriatingly, that her secret was safe with him. Carla was incensed, to the extent of challenging Phil to return to Jack's office with her and have it out with him there and then.

Phil, who would sooner have faced a roaring lion than confront Jack in such a fashion, patted her arm in male chauvinist fashion.

"Methinks the lady doth protest too much," he quoted sardonically, and, suddenly wary of the furious glint in her eye, made garbled excuses and dashed off.

Carla, goaded beyond prudence, stormed back into Jack's office.

"About that commission," she began, heedless of the fact that Jack's head was bowed in concentration over some correspondence. He looked up menacingly, very much the boss.

"Yes?" he enquired smoothly.

"In about five minutes it will be all round the shop that you docked Phil's sale out of favouritism to me."

"So what? I didn't, as it happens, and you know it."

"Would you consider changing your decision? Please?"

"Certainly not. Townsend is haphazard and careless. He was bound to slip up sooner or later. This way he won't do it again in a hurry."

"Jack, I know all that, but can't you see the position you're putting me in? The whole thing will get horribly distorted and everyone will get the wrong idea."

"What wrong idea?"

"Well ... that you ... that you and I ... er –

"Too late. They all think that anyway. You haven't got your ear to the ground, sweetheart. I'm afraid it didn't escape notice that I spent the night in your apartment recently. The grapevine has you and me in the throes of an affair. Nothing either of us can do will unconvince people now."

"You're not serious!"

"Don't be naive, Carla. This place is like a village, rife with intrigue. Why worry? Surely you'd rather have them believing something nice and natural and normal than suspecting the truth – whatever that is."

Carla, who had spent a miserable three days languishing from Jack's lack of attention, and perversely missing the favours she had so lately rebuffed, was provoked beyond endurance.

"I'm terribly sorry," she said frostily, "if my phobia about thunderstorms has subjected you to any embarrassing rumours."

"Forget it, sugar," he drawled, returning to his papers. "Who cares?"

"I care! And I suspect you do, too, given that you've been avoiding me ever since that night."

Jack looked up at her quizzically.

"You mean you noticed?" he mocked, with the ghost of a smile. Carla, cornered, didn't answer.

"You mean you actually missed me?" he taunted her mercilessly, enjoying himself now as dull colour suffused her cheeks.

"Why do things always have to be – so fraught between us?" she stammered, confused.

"They needn't be. Just say the word."

"Stop insinuating."

"Stop fishing."

For a moment they glared at each other, Jack fighting the desire to laugh, Carla that to cry.

"Say," he began at length, breaking the tension.

111

"How about coming with me this afternoon to look over an old shack? Till you keep that promise to help with my Italian, I need a guide. It's way up in the hills somewhere. We'll need to stop and ask the local peasants the way."

He flung some property details across the table.

"You don't have to take me just to be nice to me," she faltered. "You can manage perfectly well on your own."

"When I decide to be nice to you," he countered, "you'll know all about it. Now beat it. Go make a sale."

Chapter Six

Oddly enough, once Carla had resigned herself to the inevitable rumours about her relationship with Jack, it gave her an unexpected sense of freedom, of reckless-ness even. She didn't, for once, feel self-conscious at being seen driving out of the complex with him the next afternoon. It was somehow exhilarating to think that people believed them to be lovers. On reflection, per-haps this was because she *did* prefer them to believe something 'nice and normal and natural' about her, even if they did regard her as just the latest in a long line of conquests. She was abroad, far from home, with people she would probably never meet again. She found herself half-wishing their assumptions were true. In fantasy, of course, not in fact.

Jack, out of a sense of self-preservation, had decided henceforth to let Carla make the running. Avoiding her had been hell. More than anything else, he had quite simply missed her company. He wouldn't have stuck this place five minutes if she hadn't been here. The job itself bored him, he could run Catalina blindfold. Ben would have been the last person to expect Jack to take over personally, and the first person to guess just why he had done so.

Glad to have escaped the complex for an afternoon, Jack chatted amiably to Carla as they drove away from the coast, deep into the Tuscan countryside. They inevitably got lost and Carla had to ask the way several times. According to a local farmer's wife who redirected them, the cottage they had come to view had been empty for months, the elderly tenant having died and the owner lacking money for renovation.

Indeed, when they finally found the place, they both collapsed into gales of laughter. Anything less like the eight-roomed villa of their last expedition could scarcely be imagined. A sprawling, dilapidated farmhouse, overgrown with creeper, its neglected acreage tended piecemeal by neighbouring farmers since the occupant's death, it was indeed a sorry sight. But its isolated position and stunning views were worth the journey, and, as Carla reminded Jack, it *was* full of character. Full of other things too, she teased. Spiders and fieldmice and woodworm and probably death-watch beetle to boot.

They inspected the kitchen, with its old-fashioned range and huge chimney, the cramped living quarters, the large storage areas, and the rickety outbuildings. Then they climbed the creaking staircase, which wobbled underfoot, and surveyed the sleeping accommodation with its sloping ceilings. Strange scurrying noises could be heard in the roof space.

"Mmm," muttered Jack. "What do you reckon?"

"I don't," laughed Carla. "And I don't think you do either. What you might call the sublime to the ridiculous. I can't imagine you wanting to rough it in an isolated place like this."

"That's where you could be wrong," he said with a smile, looking out of the window at the tranquil landscape. "Periodically, I like to disappear for a while. Recharge my batteries. Get back in touch with myself."

Carla didn't take this too seriously. Jack was a creature of constant activity, of challenge, of glamour. Jack

114

would be bored witless in a place like this. Jokingly, she spoke her thoughts aloud. He gave her a searching look.

"What makes you so sure you know me so well?" he asked, beaming blue light into her eyes. "What makes you think you really know the first thing about me?"

She didn't answer immediately. For somehow, their eyes had locked together and Carla was suddenly aware of the silent seclusion of the place pressing in around them. The air in the room felt very still, oppressively quiet. A silence like that was dangerous, lethal. It begged for something more than words. Bravely, Carla looked back at Jack, her mouth dry, willing him to reach out and touch her, to surrender to the magnetic tug pulling at the space between them. But he didn't move.

"Well?" he asked blandly, prompting her answer.

"I think," she answered slowly, smiling secretly to herself, "that I know you about as well as you really know me."

He considered this reply for some time, thrusting his hands firmly into his pockets, steadfastly ignoring the message in her eyes. The floor was kind of hard, he told himself, and none too clean. In any case, if she was giving him the come-on, and it sure as hell looked like it, it was probably just to test him, it couldn't be for real. He turned away.

"Time we made a move," he said abruptly, bending his tall frame to descend the squeaking staircase while Carla followed, her high-heel slingbacks sticking between the gaping timbers. He had just reached the bottom of the stairs when her heel finally jammed and she tripped, falling headlong into his arms.

Jack tilted her head back none too gently and glared at her.

"Did you do that deliberately?" he asked pointedly,

almost angrily.

"Yes," she admitted, taken aback, his unexpected insight jolting her into honesty.

Tenderly, but with a kind of controlled violence, Jack gave in and kissed her, expecting to have to coax a response out of her gradually, to wear down her defences. He misjudged her totally. Afterwards, it seemed to him as if a long-buried bomb had gone off in his hands.

Unbeknown to him, Carla had relived that first kiss, the one on the balcony, more times than she would care to admit. This one was better, much, much better, because this time she didn't fight it. She was too tired to fight any more.

It was worth the wait. Drugged with the fusion of their mouths, their shared breath, she responded with a fervour that pulled painfully at the frayed threads of Jack's self-control. The kiss went as far as it could possibly go, a simulated coupling so intense in its fierce spontaneity that they lost all sense of time and place, locked together in splendid isolation, oblivious of everything except the overpowering sensations that were conspiring to weld them into one.

Carla completely lost her head. Everything she had denied and evaded in herself for so long, all her self-loathing, all her self-inflicted penance, hurtled off downhill like a runaway carriage while she raced on up the mountain track. She clung to Jack for strength, for support, for courage, pressing her body against his, exultant in her fear of what must follow. His hands disbelievingly reached underneath her loose shift and released her full breasts, caressing them into startled response. Then Carla moaned and, to Jack's amazement, started unbuckling his belt.

"Carla, honey," began Jack, so unprepared for such a response as to be almost hesitant. She didn't reply,

116

kissing the bare skin of his chest, her hands pushing his shirt away from his shoulders.

Controlling every natural instinct he possessed, Jack caught hold of her arms and immoblised her. With any other woman he would have seized the moment unquestioningly, the exchange of sexual pleasure as natural and uncomplicated to him as eating or drinking. But not with Carla. Not with a girl who until this moment had been cool to the point of frigidity. Not with a girl who turned from ice to fire in your hands. Not with a girl as damned unpredictable as this one.

"Carla!" he said roughly. "This is for real. For pity's sake don't expect me to stop, I'm not a goddammed masochist."

For reply she gave him a look so explicit, so smouldering, so womanly, that no man on earth could have resisted her. Why not? Jack asked himself, looking at her soft, warm mouth, her eyes glazed with desire, her body pliant and yielding in his arms. Why the hell not?

Throwing their discarded clothes over the bare floorboards, he pulled her down on the makeshift couch, reminding himself to hold back a bit, to be gentle, sensitive, considerate. But Carla was on a rollercoaster ride he could barely keep up with. Her hunger strike over, she was greedy from starvation. She clung to him shamelessly, wantonly, arousing, responding, sharing, giving, demanding, until her body, shuddering with fulfilment, could take no more.

Afterwards, they lay silent for a long time. Something wasn't quite right, thought Jack uneasily, holding her close and feeling a gradual but unmistakable tension replace her satiated languor.

"Something the matter?" he asked at last. "Are you cold?"

Carla nodded. Wordlessly retrieving items of clothing, she started jerkily putting them back on. She felt weak, dazed, other-worldly, like someone waking up from a particularly vivid dream. She stole a furtive glance at Jack. He had the disbelieving air of a man who had just jumped off a cliff and landed safely in the sea.

"What is it, honey?" he repeated. Heck, if she wasn't satisfied after *that*—

"Nothing," she muttered, suddenly shy, turning her back on him as she dressed.

"We'll be black and blue tomorrow," teased Jack. "This floor sure is hard. I very nearly turned you down on account of it."

Carla's smile was tight-lipped.

"I didn't give you much of a chance to do that, did I?" she asked dryly, handing him his shirt. "Can we go back now?"

Jack sighed, exasperated, as they both finished dressing.

"Carla, I give up, I give in, you've got me beat. For God's sake, give me the crossword solution so we can play a more interesting game."

"No need. You solved it all by yourself. You just found out all the answers. No more surprises. It wasn't nearly as hard as you thought, was it?"

"Just what are you driving at?" he demanded, taking in the painful flush staining her face and neck. "You surely aren't going to tell me now that you regret what happened? That you're ashamed of it in some way?"

Carla looked away.

"Sweetheart," he persisted, frustrated, "you enjoyed every minute of it and so did I. The sooner we find a nice comfortable bed and repeat the experience the better. Don't make a big production out of it."

"Oh no," bit back Carla, "I won't make a 'big production' out of it. This is strictly fringe, I know. Off-off-off-off Broadway."

"Give me strength!" exploded Jack. "What's got into you? You want me to marry you?"

But Carla had already clammed up. She strode out of the house and into the car and hardly spoke another word all the way back to Catalina.

Back in her apartment, Carla stood beneath the shower, soaping away the dust of ancient floorboards, the tears running down her face and mingling with the soothing, tepid water. Quite why she was crying she did not know. She seemed to have cried more in the last month than she had in several years. Self-pity, she thought. That was the usual reason. She looked down at her body miserably, remembering the ecstasy of that afternoon, contemplating the agony that must follow and cursing herself for her weakness.

It was not Jack's technique, practised though it was, that had achieved the apparent miracle. It was not his expert hands, his passionate lips, or his undoubted virility. Jack was an accomplished lover, but he was not unique. It had taken more than his sexual expertise to work the miracle, more than skilled lovemaking to release the trapped wanton in her. She had responded that way to a man before and regretted it ever since. Knowing what she knew about herself, nothing would have induced her to play with fire again, not when there was a safe hearth at home with Remo which remained cold and unlit.

It was quite simple. She had gone temporarily insane. She had lost control, for the first time in years, and broken out of her secret prison for one reason, and one reason only. Because she had finally managed to achieve the impossible, the one thing she had staked her salvation on. The one thing she had hoped to do eventually with a man who didn't exist – or rather with a man she still hadn't met, and probably never would.

Certainly, emphatically, not with Jack Fitzgerald.

But she had done it all the same. Spectacularly, secretly, and hopelessly, she had finally fallen in love.

Despite the briefness of her acquaintance with Jack, she knew him well enough by now to be able to bank on one or two things. After today, he would no longer take no for an answer. What had just happened between them was no casual, ships-in-the-night encounter. Certainly not for her, whose emotions were enmeshed to a frightening degree. And not for him either, though for very different reasons. Carla might lack Jack's experience, but she was perfectly well aware that the explosive lovemaking they had shared was something quite out of the ordinary. Jack knew when he was on to a good thing. He would be ready for a very thorough, very exhaustive affair with her before he finally moved on. When it suited him, when the gloss wore off, unscathed, undamaged, it would be "So long, honey" and she would be filed away in his memory as a 'fantastic piece of ass' along with perhaps half a dozen others who stood out from the numberless throng.

Jack, as Helen had warned her, didn't understand the first thing about love. It didn't fit in with his freewheeling life style. Jack was blithely unaware of his own strength. Without in the least meaning to, he would smash her heart to pieces.

The choice was simple enough. She could make the most of the affair while it lasted, and trust her acting abilities not to give the game away. Or she could break it off right now, before she got in too deep. There was another option, but she refused even to consider it. It was completely out of the question.

Meanwhile Jack, also under the shower, had the stricken feeling of one who has got all the answers right and still failed the exam. Normally, he reminded himself, he gave a wide berth to women with hang-ups.

Helen's singular lack of neurosis had been the secret of her remarkable staying power. Jack needed a woman like Carla like he needed a bed of nails. She was precisely the type he usually avoided – complicated, uptight, over-emotional. The ideal woman was a soft drug, a nice safe high, strictly non-addictive. Carla de Luca was pure heroin. One shot of her and you were hooked. He must be out of his mind.

Carla's telephone gave out the double bleep. Eyes red from weeping, she picked the receiver up.

"Your place or mine?" mocked Jack.

"Please, Jack. I have a headache."

"Not already? I thought only married women got those."

"I mean it,"

"Carla, I'm coming over right now and we're going to have this out once and for all. Whatever the hell I did to upset you, I'm truly sorry, and if you'll just tell me what it was then I'll avoid doing it again. Just don't pile on the agony like I raped you or something, okay?"

He hung up, and seconds later was on the doorstep.

Carla was still dishevelled from her shower, barefooted and in a bathwrap. Jack was already dressed to go out.

"Put some clothes on," he ordered. "Let's get out of this place to eat."

Too numb to argue, she went obediently into the bedroom to get dressed. He followed her and sat down on the bed.

"Please, Jack," she protested, embarrassed.

"I hate to shock you, honey," he replied calmly, "but I'm blessed with total recall. I can remember every detail of that gorgeous body in glorious technicolor, so it's dumb for you to act all coy, especially as I'm going to be spending most of tonight making love to you. With

121

the light *on*."

He reached over and slipped the bathrobe from her shoulders.

"God, you're beautiful," he murmured, as Carla blushed scarlet. "Heaven only knows what you're so ashamed of."

Carla began dressing in a hurry while Jack reminded himself that she wasn't in the mood, that he was very hungry, and that they had plenty of time. There was no point in pushing her. You couldn't rush a volcano.

Jack had located a quiet, expensive restaurant with secluded booths, probably a favoured meeting place for the local adulterers.

"Don't drink too much," he admonished, keeping an eye on her glass. "I don't want you falling asleep on me."

Carla, for once, had little appetite, picking at her escalope and tearing pieces of bread into tiny fragments.

"Okay," Jack said finally, when she rejected dessert in favour of coffee. "Give. And make it good."

Carla's eyes remained downcast.

"I still can't figure it out," he continued patiently. "You weren't a virgin – that much, if you don't mind my saying so, was obvious. So you can't be having some kind of moral crisis over that. You enjoyed it, I won't elaborate on that. I enjoyed it, in case you didn't notice. We're both free, so no-one's going to get hurt. Or are we? Is there a guy back home? Is that it?"

He couldn't see her face at all, it was downcast and completely shrouded by her hair. She shook her head.

"Don't tell me," sighed Jack, "You're afraid you've given me an anti-social disease."

That did the trick.

"Don't be insulting!" fumed Carla, stung into response.

"Heck, Carla, where's your sense of humour? Oh

God, I've got it. You're not on the pill. Why didn't you say? I would have—"

"Oh, for goodness' sake," she muttered sullenly, "I don't get caught that way twice," and bit her tongue.

"Uh-huh," mused Jack, looking at her quizzically. "So I *was* on the right track that day at the villa?"

Hovering on the brink of confession, Carla quite lost her tongue.

"You think I'm going to sit in judgment on you?" he prompted. "Want to hear a few of my sins first?"

"All right," said Carla finally, in a low voice. "But not in here."

"It's a deal," said Jack, signalling for the bill. "Tell me later. Tell me in bed."

He didn't press it further, waiting for her to choose her own moment. They would never get anywhere, that was for sure, until she had got it all off her chest. He felt strangely responsible for whatever this other guy had done to her, experiencing an unfamiliar urge to be unselfish, patient, protective, increasingly aware as time went on that he was getting too involved with this girl for his own good. Or hers.

He could tell by her eyes that her burden oppressed her. She was silent in the car going back, and wavered slightly on the threshold of her apartment before letting him in. Once inside, she looked at him helplessly, wordlessly imploring him to take charge. Her mind raced and faltered, caught up in the conflict of prudence versus instinct.

He made it easier for her by not asking questions. He simply undressed her slowly, seductively, removing her mental armour along with her clothes. Then he laid her gently on the bed and prepared to join her there. Carla found she couldn't take her eyes off him. Unblushingly, punch-drunk with warring emotions, she watched him discard each garment, mesmerised, feasting on the sheer male beauty of him. He lay down beside her and cradled her head against his chest.

"You got pregnant, right?" he said softly.

Carla nodded, biting her lip, wishing she could trust herself, desperately wishing that she could trust Jack. After an endless pause at last she found her voice.

"I grew up painfully aware that I wasn't a pretty child. By my teens it had become an obsession. I was always the ugly duckling, as I told you, and then I went through the spotty stage, and the puppy fat stage, and so on. So you can imagine, I had very little confidence in myself.

"My father was a kind man, but terribly old-fashioned, very strict, the whole Catholic Italian bit. I was educated in a Convent school and by today's standards I was almost totally ignorant about sex, apart from the stuff the nuns taught us about tadpoles." She hesitated. Jack took hold of her hand and starting kissing her fingers one by one.

"Needless to say, I wasn't allowed to wear make-up or go out with boys, not that I got to meet any. In any case, by the time I was sixteen I was convinced that I was totally hideous, no-one would ever want to marry me, I would end up an old maid, etc, etc. In actual fact, I suppose by then I must have looked much as I do now, especially as I was rather . . . well-developed for my age. And, being adolescent, I probably had all this bottled up sex-drive just bursting to get out, although I didn't recognise it at the time.

"Well, my mother had this sort of second cousin – everybody Italian is Mamma's second cousin – Paolo, he was called. He was from my mother's village, near Naples, and he'd been writing to her for some time, asking if Pappa would give him a job. That part of Italy is very rural, very poor, and Paolo was desperately keen to come to England, learn the language, make his fortune, and so on. I expect he thought the streets would be paved with gold.

"My parents hadn't ever actually met him, and they didn't know a great deal about him, but with Mario away in the seminary Pappa needed help with the business, and Paolo was willing to work for very little. So it was agreed that he could come on a trial basis. Naturally he couldn't afford digs on what Pappa could pay him, so part of the arrangement was that he lived with us.

"My parents, looking back, must have been very naive. They gave me the job of teaching cousin Paolo English, which of course gave us carte blanche to spend a lot of time together. Given the state of mind I was in, I was ready to fall in love with just about anyone, let alone a hunk like Paolo. He was about twenty-five, and very good-looking in a Latin-lover kind of way. Needless to say, he was the first man who'd ever paid me any attention, and certainly the only one who looked on me as a woman, unlike Mamma and Pappa, who still thought of me as a child and couldn't imagine that anything would go on under their own roof with someone who was 'family'.

"So, you've guessed it, while the rest of the family sat downstairs watching television, Paolo and I were busy not studying English up in his bedroom. It must seem odd to you, that a man of that age would mess about with the resident adolescent instead of finding himself a proper girlfriend. But then you have to remember that Paolo hardly spoke any English, he didn't have much money to spend, and it probably didn't take him long to work out that I was going to be a pushover.

"He knew the line to take with a nice girl like me. He didn't pounce on me, far from it. We used to talk for hours, in Italian, about everything under the sun.

Even though I was terribly shy, and had this huge inferiority complex, I sort of blossomed under all the attention he gave me. Then he started telling me that I was *bella, bella*. That he'd never met a girl like me before, that he couldn't bear the thought of leaving me, that I was the only woman he'd ever loved, and that one day he wanted to marry me and take me back to Italy with him. But because I was still at school, and because he was still so poor, we would have to keep our plans secret for the moment, until I was a bit older and he'd managed to save some money for our future together.

"I believed every word. I was in heaven, it was a dream come true. I was so pathetically *grateful* to him for loving me. So when he finally moved in for the kill, I never even thought to resist him. I would have done anything for him. I was totally immature and utterly infatuated. And so, while my parents thought Paolo was learning English, he was busy teaching me something quite different."

Carla faltered, ashamed. "He was a pretty good teacher, come to that. Very thorough. But then he had such a willing pupil."

Her voice dried, and Jack knew that the worst was yet to come.

"The kind of precautions Paolo took were rather rudimentary, as approved by the Vatican. Self-control wasn't his strong point, and so naturally I got pregnant. I was three months gone before I even realised what was wrong with me.

"In a way, I was pleased, excited. I thought it would mean getting married straight away. When I told Paolo he didn't, to his credit, bat an eyelid. He must have been one jump ahead of me. He told me not to tell my Mamma, or go to the doctor just yet, he would talk to Pappa and handle everything.

"Then one day I got home from school to find that

126

Paolo had had to go back to Italy suddenly. Mamma told me he'd had bad news from home, but would be coming back. He'd left me a note under my pillow. It said that he'd had word that his mother was very ill and was asking for him. He hoped not to be gone long, and would write to me again soon.

"So I waited, and waited, and there wasn't a word from him. I didn't dare tell my parents what had happened, but my pregnancy was starting to show, and I knew it wouldn't be long before Mamma noticed. So I wrote to him, in Italian of course, asking after his mother and saying that I would soon have to tell my parents about the baby. I asked him if he would write to Pappa explaining that we would be getting married. I told him I loved him desperately and couldn't wait to see him again. The usual outpourings.

"I got a reply, but not from Paolo. I got a reply from his wife. Mother of his two legitimate *bambini* back home. You can imagine what the letter said. It was a sort of verbal equivalent of scratching my eyes out. She told me to look after my bastard myself, and called me what my mother called me when I finally told her I was pregnant: *puttana*. That means whore, by the way, you won't find it in your phrase book. Mamma was totally hysterical, I thought she was going to kill me. Pappa just went very quiet, very white, he wouldn't even speak to me. I think they would have been less upset if I had died.

"Abortion was out of the question, of course, on religious grounds, even though they were desperate to keep my condition a secret, especially from my younger sisters. I think Gabby must have guessed – she was about twelve at the time – but of course nothing was ever said in front of the children. They had some plan to export me to a distant aunt, as in all the best novels, till I'd had the baby, and then it was going to be adopted.

I wasn't given any say in the matter. As far as they were concerned I was just pregnant, as if that wasn't bad enough. No one seemed to realise that the reason I went completely to pieces wasn't because I was pregnant, it was because I'd been betrayed."

She stopped, fighting the tremor in her voice, the pricking of tears in her eyes.

"Honey," Jack whispered, "it's the oldest, saddest story in the world. Nothing to punish yourself for. Happens every day . . ."

"I haven't finished," Carla interrupted. The words came faster, toneless, dead, flat, the only way she could bear to say them.

"Mamma had got these pills from the doctor to tide her over her troubles. Some sort of tranquilliser, I suppose. She kept them in the bathroom cabinet. It was so terribly easy. I took the whole bottle.

"Suicide's a mortal sin, you know, and so is murder, but then I was in Hell already. I planned it very well, I meant it to work. I thought it would be nice and painless, no need for courage, the traditional coward's way out. I took the pills after everyone else was in bed, safe in the knowledge that I'd be dead when they woke up. I would have been, too, except that the pain of the miscarriage woke me up before they had a chance to work. Gabby heard me moaning and got the fright of her life, poor kid.

"It was all too much for Pappa. His heart gave out a week later."

Her eyes were vacant, hollow. Jack was silent, holding her very tight.

"Don't you see?" she wept at last. "Don't you see?"

Jack saw. The oldest natural urge in the world cultivated in a hothouse and then left out in the frost. No wonder it had only survived one season.

"Pappa dying," continued Carla jerkily, "wrecked my

mother's life, and my sisters', emotionally and financially. Mamma adored him, we all did. I know what you're going to say: he would have died anyway. I've tried to tell myself that a thousand times, but I still feel I killed him. He was such a sweet man, Jack, so devoted to all of us. And I let him down so badly. He was too ill to speak while he was dying. I never knew whether he'd been able to forgive me."

She gave in to the tears then, and Jack remembered, and at last understood, the excessive, stormy weeping on the day of Ben's collapse. He let her cry until she was ready to continue. There was nothing useful he could say.

"I think that was why I became an actress," she finally managed to say. "It was a means of escape. I could never get over the feeling of guilt, of self-loathing. I developed an obsessive fear of my own sexuality, it became an out-and-out phobia. I was never, ever, going to risk humiliating myself again. I was going to play it safe. The easiest way to lose myself was by becoming someone else. I don't mean just on the stage, either. Little by little, I consciously changed my personality to what you saw that day in Maxwell's: hard, tough, smart, confident and cold. It was like armourplating, to stop anyone getting too near the real me. And it worked. Until . . . until today."

The full impact of her confession finally hit him. Dear God, thought Jack suddenly, with a stab of insight, what have I done? Carla, realising that she was in danger of giving herself away completely, fell silent.

"Carla . . ." Jack began with difficulty. "The last thing in the world I want to do is hurt you some more. You . . . you haven't got hold of any damn fool notion, have you, that you – that you're in love with *me*?"

From any other man than Jack the question would have sounded conceited, arrogant even. As it was, the

129

words came out humbly, honestly, full of concern and intuition. Carla, steeling herself, remembered just in time that she was supposed to be an actress. And knew that to cry off their relationship now, as she had considered doing, would only confirm his worst suspicions and make her seem totally pathetic. Make him feel guilty. Worst of all, make him feel sorry for her. She looked him full in the face, her eyes bright with deceit and pride.

"Jack, I'm a whole lot older and wiser now. You happened to come along at the right time and in the right place, that's all. I'm a thousand miles from home and you're a very attractive man. This is chemistry, not romance. A good – a *few* good – love affairs are just what I need. Look upon yourself as a pioneer."

Her face turned from tragedy to comedy as completely as if she had just switched theatrical masks. She smiled at him sweetly, almost coquettishly.

Jack looked back at her searchingly. Her eyes didn't waver. Then, finally convinced, he grinned with relief.

"Seems to me," he murmured, nibbling teasingly at an earlobe, "that the first thing we have to do is to replace all those bad memories with some good ones. You know I can never resist a challenge. This Paolo must have been quite a guy, in his way. Was he a very good lover?"

He moved his attention to the sensitive hollow of her throat, his tongue sending delicious shivers down her back.

"I suppose so," admitted Carla, blushing. "But then, I was only sixteen, and I've never had anyone to compare him with."

Jack smiled a forgivably complacent smile.

"You go right ahead, honey," he invited her softly, "and compare him with me."

Chapter Seven

But you can't compare a helicopter ride with a trip to the moon. Paolo faded further into insignificance every time Jack made love to her. Which was frequently, lingeringly, expertly. And then Jack was so many lovers in one. Gentle and comforting, passionate and demanding, playful and funny. He moved into Carla's apartment with his usual disregard for discretion. He spent every spare moment with her, and everyone knew it. Although they both did their best not to let their affair disrupt their working relationship with each other, or anyone else, inevitably it distanced both of them from the rest of the team. Particularly Ian McIntyre who, once an accredited war hero, now ranked little better than a deserter.

Carla tried to take the mature woman's view of the situation. Rather abashed at her sudden status as a *femme fatale*, she endeavoured to think herself into just that rôle, telling herself that she wasn't really in love at all, that she was just making up for lost time with a man who happened to be irresistible in bed. By the end of the summer, things would have burnt themselves out. By the time Jack was ready to call it a day, she would be, too. She would return to real life having come to terms with herself, perhaps even ready to re-evaluate the possibility of marriage to Remo. If she could tell most of the truth to Jack, a man she'd only just met, then surely she could trust Remo, whom she'd known for years, with all of it?

She tried, cold-bloodedly, to imagine making love with Remo, but the images wouldn't come. Her mind was too saturated with Jack, her body too totally possessed by his to contemplate intimacy with any other man.

Time passed and things did not cool off, quite the contrary. What might have started off as a natural urge, a long-denied desire, was becoming for Carla a need so intense as to be compulsive. Her compulsion had its roots in fear: fear of pain, fear of loss, fear of the truth.

Jack, too, was afraid. For the first time in his life, he was getting inexorably involved to a degree he had never intended. He had made love to a great many women. Most of them, by his choice, had been around, were fashionably uninhibited and knew from long practice how to please a man. But Carla's capacity for passion was something else altogether. No wonder, he thought, she had been so afraid to acknowledge it. She aroused him in a way he had not experienced before, and increasingly he could not bear to think of another man touching her. Jealousy and possessiveness had never been his style, but Carla had become, in her damaged innocence, so totally his that he found himself suffering the very same inadmissible but unmistakable emotions he had so decried in others.

These secret depths of feeling were never admitted, let alone discussed, and the holding back found release in pointless, petty quarrels that began to flare up suddenly out of nothing at all. Unaccountably, Jack announced one day that he had made up his mind to buy the deserted farmhouse up in the hills – as he had a perfect right to do, of course. There was no reason why he should seek Carla's approval in the matter, but they were spoiling for a fight about something, anything.

"I just don't understand," she wailed, "what on earth you want with a ramshackle place in the middle of nowhere. If I were buying a house in Tuscany, I'd pick somewhere more civilised, more central. It's a long way from the beach, miles from the airport—"

"It's got what I want," said Jack shortly. "I told you, I get itchy for peace and quiet once in a while. Anyone would think I was asking you to live in it."

"Just as well you're *not*," retorted Carla, stung. "Seeing as I wouldn't even consider it."

"And just what is that supposed to mean?" he taunted her. "You wouldn't consider what, exactly?"

Carla hesitated, rattled. "It was just a manner of speaking," she snapped crossly. This was typical, she thought, of their increasing tendency to bicker about the slightest thing. Inevitable, of course. Sooner or later there would be a showdown, a nice big bust-up, and they would go their separate ways.

"Hypothetically speaking," continued Jack calmly, "just what *would* you say if I asked you to come and live with me?"

"I'd say thank you but no," said Carla with deliberate flippancy.

"Marriage or nothing, huh?"

She sighed heavily. "Don't delude yourself, Jack. Just because I . . . just because we . . ."

"Just because we're terrific in the sack?" His voice was cool, provocative.

"Must you use those crude Americanisms?"

"Beg your pardon, ma'am. I thought that was a pretty polite way of putting it."

"Jack, let's drop this conversation, shall we? If you want to buy this house, go ahead and buy it. It's your money."

"Thank you kindly for your permission," said Jack dryly. "Perhaps you'd ring up a surveyor for me and get it checked out."

"Do it yourself. You're quite capable."

"I don't want them thinking they're dealing with a sucker foreigner with more money than sense. Tell them you're my wife. That'll keep them on their toes."

"Won't that cause of a bit of confusion when the real Mrs Fitzgerald comes to stay?"

"The real Mrs Fitzgerald?"

"Helen."

It was the first time since their affair had begun that Carla had ever mentioned her name. A dozen times it had hovered on her lips and been bitten back.

"Helen? She's my brother's widow, not my wife."

"Don't split hairs. You know exactly what I mean."

"Sure I know what you mean," mocked Jack, seizing her shoulders, his face a picture of mischief. "You're jealous. It must be the Italian in you coming out."

"Of course I'm not jealous of Helen. If anything, I'm jealous *for* her. How do you think she must feel, being picked up and dropped again like a well-thumbed book. I don't know why she puts up with you."

"Pure self-interest," responded Jack impassively. "On both sides. Helen's got her eyes wide open. She always did have. She was looking for some action long before Steve died. I wouldn't like you thinking I took advantage of a poor bereaved woman. They had a God-awful miserable marriage. They were both playing the field for a couple of years before Steve got killed."

"You have a wonderful talent for self-justification. The poor woman thinks you're going to marry her in the end."

"Now what the hell gave you an idea like that?"

"She did," Carla bit her lip. Perhaps, on reflection, that was less than fair on Helen. "She gave me a bit of advice that day I drove her to the airport. She said, if I remember, 'Play it for laughs, kiddo, but don't get in too deep. He always comes back to me in the end.' Or words to that effect."

"So she didn't actually mention marriage."

"Well, not exactly," Carla admitted reluctantly. "But that's obviously what she's got in mind. You ought to marry her. She'd at least put up with your affairs."

"Meaning you wouldn't?"

"The question doesn't arise, as I'm not the one you'd be marrying."

"Okay, it's a hypothetical question not a proposal. How *would* you view my 'affairs'?"

Carla, having talked herself into a corner, hid her discomfiture with a peal of mocking laughter.

"Need you ask?" she demanded skittishly. "Like you said, I'm an Italian!"

"Meaning?" quizzed Jack, eyes gleaming.

"That I'd probably commit murder. You first, then her."

Jack took her face in his hands and studied her expression intently.

"I do believe you would," he said thoughtfully.

"And how about you?" Carla challenged him, going on the attack. "How would *you* react if your wife was unfaithful?"

"It would all depend," said Jack levelly, "on who my wife turned out to be."

"Well, I think it's high time you got married," pursued Carla recklessly, determined to goad him. "You're turning into some sort of ageing Peter Pan."

"Peter Pan, huh? Well, at least he could fly. Which is more than you can say for most of the poor dumb married bastards. Or the poor dumb divorced bastards, come to that. Alimony, custody battles, ulcers, I can live without them."

135

"You'll be lonely when you're old. You'll wish you had a family. You'll regret not having children."

"Kids are for keeping women happy. They leave me cold. Mostly they're spoilt little monsters."

"Any child of yours probably would be a monster!"

"Want to make one together just to prove us both right? What's got into you, Carla? What's with all the heavy analysis? When I think I need it, I'll go find me a shrink like everyone else."

"Oh, I see," spat Carla. "You can do the amateur Freud bit on me, but if *I* point out a few home truths about you, you start acting paranoid!"

"What home truths, for God's sake? I'm all up front. I'm simple. I have no dark secrets, no hidden depths. Have I?"

The question was oddly inflected, like a riddle. But Carla was beyond subtlety.

"You might have, if you bothered to look inside yourself!" she blazed. "If you weren't so . . . so self-satisfied, if everything didn't come so *easy* for you. Money, women, status, you've got it all, and what you haven't got comes as soon as you snap your fingers. You've never had to struggle for anything, you're the first one to admit it. You're brash, and shallow, and . . . and . . . you don't know what it is to *suffer*!"

"Terrific opinion you've got of me," observed Jack mildly. "Perhaps if I was as uptight and insecure as you, you'd like me better."

"I am *not* uptight and insecure!"

"No kidding? You sure had me fooled."

"You just rub me up the wrong way, that's all," sulked Carla, retreating ungraciously. "In fact, when you think about it, we haven't got much in common, have we?"

"Oh, I don't know. We get by," His voice was heavy with exasperated amusement. He reached for her hungrily.

"Honestly, Jack! Don't you ever think about anything else but sex?"

"I thought I spent all my time thinking about money. Make up your mind, sweetheart."

"I'm fed up with this argument."

"That's because you're losing."

"Naturally. You always have to win, don't you."

"If it bugs you so much, go find yourself a loser. The world's full of them, Go find yourself a nice, sensitive, soft-hearted guy who'll let you walk all over him."

If Jack had met Remo, or even known about him, he couldn't have described him more succinctly. Carla reacted as angrily as if he had named him.

"Perhaps I will! At least he wouldn't treat me like a sex object!"

"Is that how you feel with me? I never noticed you complaining."

Disconcerted, Jack saw that Carla's eyes were brimming with unshed tears.

"Carla, honey, I didn't start this fight. And now you're crying like I was a brute or something. Come on. Let's go to bed."

"No! You just use bed as a way of simplifying everything."

"You want it to be complicated? I thought the deal was that we had lots of fun and no-one got hurt?"

"Then perhaps it's time we stopped having fun before somebody does get hurt."

"Carla, you're dramatising again. It's a bad habit and it's time you kicked it. You've been overworking and this place is getting to you. It's claustrophobic. Let's have ourselves a week off. Let's drive across to France, have a change of air. Come on, what do you say?"

Carla, sniffing and suddenly child-like, found herself sorely tempted.

"I can't afford to take a week off," she said sullenly.

"Have you any idea of how much I make in a week?"

"Sure I have. No problem, I'll make it up to you. We'll work out your average and give you a week's holiday pay."

"You most certainly will not. I wouldn't dream of accepting unearned money from you."

"Okay, I'll give *everyone* a week off with pay, or money in lieu. Satisfied? Knowing that lot, they'll all take the money in lieu. Come to that, you can too. Fair's fair. Which is it to be? An extra slice of cake, or a week off with me?"

"If I choose the former . . ." said Carla slowly,

". . . I'll accuse you of thinking only about money."

"And if I choose the latter . . ."

". . . I'll accuse you," smiled Jack, "of thinking only about sex."

When Carla worked out just how many million lire it had cost Jack to buy off her scruples, it gave her considerable food for thought. Money, in itself, was clearly meaningless to him. It was simply a yardstick of success, an instrument of power. He spent it as easily as he made it, and rumour had it he gave sizeable sums away, anonymously, to charity. She had prodded him about this once, but he had neatly rebuffed the question. And so, weighing all this up, she managed to swallow her initial discomfiture at the money he proceeded to spend on her, at the size and splendour of the suite he had booked at the Hotel du Sud in St Raphael, and resigned herself to choosing the most expensive and exotic dishes on every menu.

It was all very much like you might imagine the ultimate in honeymoons, thought Carla, except, of course, that they weren't married. They both felt more relaxed away from Catalina. The self-destruct element Carla had been building into their relationship, the rows she had been unconsciously generating to hasten its demise, receded in the unfamiliar holiday atmosphere. Jack, observing this change in her, breathed a sigh of relief. No tears, no tension, was luxury indeed. He felt less trapped, less compromised. Like her, he shed his defences. And it cleared his thinking in the most miraculous way.

It was a week of lazy, decadent days and tender, passionate nights. Carla, resigned to a broken heart at the end of it, told herself she might as well be hanged for a sheep as a lamb. She let go completely, released everything she had been holding in reserve, threw caution to the winds. The results of this abandon were, for both of them, so far-reaching that instinctively they dared not speak of it. They would lie silently together, exhausted, entwined, shattered, saying nothing, thinking their own private thoughts.

If only, thought Carla, if only ... Jack as a lover and Jack as a man were two very different propositions. As a lover he was caring, intuitive, and in a strange way vulnerable, dependent even. He never tried to hide the power she had over him, or would have had over him, had she tried to deny him what she gave so unstintingly. But as a man Jack was, she knew, unyielding, unsentimental, self-sufficient, driven by the desire for success, shrinking from emotional ties. The anchors of life were, for him, dead weights. Permanent commitments would leave him landlocked, becalmed. Generous in his freedom, he would be mean in captivity. He neither offered nor craved security. Well, this week for once, she had tried to live by Jack's code. She lived only for the day. And for the night.

On their last day in St Raphael, they had driven north away from the resort and walked for miles through the herb-scented countryside. They didn't talk much, both too preoccupied. The summer was already ripening into autumn. In a month Catalina would be sold solid, and Carla would be back in Soho, waitressing in the Isola Bella, telephone selling, hustling for a part in panto, fending off Remo ... Remo! He hadn't written. Perhaps, after all, he had found somebody else.

"Let's sit down a while," said Jack, indicating a grassy bank. "There's something I've got to say to you before we go back tomorrow."

Carla's heart gave a sudden lurch of dread. He was going, she was sure, to suggest that they cool it for a bit, explain that things were getting too involved. She had been expecting something of the kind. This last week had got out of of hand. She had been too intense, too transparent. He had worked out that she was in love with him, and he was starting to feel stifled. It had had to happen. It was no surprise. At least she was ready for the pain this time. This time, at least, no-one else would get hurt.

"Okay," she said flippantly. "Let's get it over with. I know what you're going to say."

"You do? I didn't realise I was such an open book. Care to say it for me?"

"That things are getting too heavy, man, and we oughta kinda stay loose, perhaps split for a while."

"Quit trying to take off my accent. It makes you sound like a B-movie. You've got me all wrong as usual. That wasn't what I was going to say at all."

"It wasn't?" Her imagination began galloping. Perhaps he was going to suggest setting her up in a little love-nest, a girl on tap for his trips to London. Always supposing Helen stayed at home.

"After the summer, when you go back," began Jack. "I'll be returning to the States for a few months. Thanks to Ben getting ill, I've had to leave a lot of things on ice for too long. Then I'll have to go the the West Coast, and probably Japan as well, before I get a chance to visit London again, or take advantage of the house you so disapprove of in Tuscany." He paused.

"So?" asked Carla defensively, as her first theory disintegrated. "What's new? This has got to be the longest you've ever stuck it in one place."

Jack looked at her levelly.

"Going to miss me?" he asked.

"I suppose so. At first, anyway."

"At first? You mean, until you find somebody else?"

"Don't put words in my mouth. I shall miss you at first, of course I shall. But I don't intend to spend the rest of my life moping over you, if that's what's worrying you." She began tearing distractedly at a tuft of grass.

"You don't . . . love, me, then?"

"Love you? Of course not."

"How about looking at me when you speak? I can't see your face."

"I said, of course not!" she repeated, flushing, forcing herself to meet his gaze. He took her head between his hands so that she couldn't turn away.

"Of course not what?"

"Of course I don't love you!" floundered Carla, shutting her eyes as she spoke.

"Hmmm," said Jack cryptically. "If you say so. Still, I'm not proud. Will you marry me anyway?"

To Carla, eyes still shut, his voice seemed to come from a very long way off. She opened them and looked at him, open-mouthed.

"Why?" she asked at length, weakly.

"Because you won't move in with me permanently any other way. Because I can't bear the thought of you with another man. Because I want everything out in the open with your old-fashioned folks. Because I'm hooked and I can't face the withdrawal symptoms. I want you on prescription. Well?"

Carla found that her voice had disappeared somewhere down inside her throat, the same, panicky feeling as when you dried on stage.

"What . . . sort of marriage?" she croaked eventually.

"What sort? A legalised love affair, I guess."

"What about the other things? A home. Roots. Children."

Jack lay back on the grass and squinted up at the sky.

"I don't want to shoot you any kind of line, Carla. I haven't undergone a personality change. I'm the way I always have been and the things you don't like about me aren't going to disappear just because we're married. A home – okay, as long as we have several and don't get fixated on any one place. It spooks me, the thought of getting attached to *things* – furniture, and all that stuff. Kids – eventually, sure, but not right away. You're still young, we've got plenty of time. Roots – well, I've managed just fine without them till now, and yours don't seem to have done you much good. All this repression and guilt you feel is largely down to your roots."

"You can't avoid – responsibility, by calling it guilt."

"Carla, for the last time, your father had a weak heart. He didn't drop dead just because you got pregnant. So he left your mother poor. That was his fault, not yours. Whatever mistakes you made as a kid, you've sure as hell paid for them with the best years of your life. Tell you what. We'll move your mom into a new house, and we'll do right by all your sisters. We'll get the musical one the best teachers in the business, and the teenage one a new wardrobe. I'll give the brainy one a job, and we'll shower the little one with all the toys and candy she can handle. And your brother the padre can build himself a brand new church. Will that pay off your guilt? Then you can leave them to get on with their lives while you start a new one with me. And that means where I go, you go. You can visit them all you like, but I have to come first. I'm marrying you, not your outsize family."

"My God," murmured Carla, "you really are an all-or-nothing merchant, aren't you?"

"Sooner or later," continued Jack, "I guess I'll slow down a bit. But not yet. Looking around at the people I know, marriage seems to mean boredom and instant middle age. Well, it's not going to be that way for us. Marriage is a state of mind, not a compulsory life-style. I'm marrying you, Carla, because it's the only way I can keep you. It doesn't mean I'm signing any godammed pledge."

"Pledge? You mean about other women? Because if you think I would ever stand for—"

"Not other women, dumbo! Heck, Carla, I'm not Superman. I get all I can handle with you. Then I happen to believe in the old adage about sauce for the gander. I'm not letting you near any other men, so it's only fair I don't cheat on you."

"Promises, promises."

Jack sat up, hurt at the cynical tone of her voice. It wasn't quite what he had expected. Carla, unable to cope, was reduced to stilted ad-libbing. Oh what a tangled web we weave . . .

"You're forgetting my career," she prevaricated, clutching desperately at straws.

Jack sighed. He'd forgotten about that.

"I happen to think," he pointed out with typical frankness, "that acting isn't a true vocation with you. It's more of a front, an escape. Are you sure you really need it any more?"

"Some people happen to think I have talent."

"Sure you have. You and thousands of others, all chasing the same parts. If you care that much, I told you, I've got contacts in the theatre."

"No!" exploded Carla. "I either get a part on merit

or not at all."

"You still get it on merit. I'm just talking about a routine bit of unfair advantage. It's traditional in show business. And every other kind of business, come to that."

"The loaded dice theory?"

"You've got it. Carla, we're getting too far away from the subject. I wasn't planning a ten-page contract. I want to marry you, give you everything I have, no strings. But I'm not giving out any soft soap. This is me. This is the way I am. Take it or leave it, honey."

Carla, locked deep in a private dilemma, struggled with herself while Jack looked on, perplexed. Surely to God she wasn't going to turn him down?

"I often think," she said quietly, "that we don't really know each other at all."

"We know all we have to know to pass the audition. We've got the rest of our lives to learn the script."

Carla turned her back on him, her knuckles white, gazing unseeingly at the horizon.

"Jack –" she began.

"Yes?" he whispered, taking hold of her from behind, kissing her neck and caressing her breasts.

"You see, the thing is . . . I'd rather hoped that, when I got married, I'd have a family quite soon. You see . . ."

"I know. You still feel bad about the baby, right? Sweetheart, you've got to put all that behind you now. What happened was for the best. Think about it. If you'd had the baby, you'd never be able to forget this Paolo guy. You wouldn't be able to look at the child without remembering what had happened, without feeling pain. I'm *glad* you haven't got another man's child. However wicked or selfish it sounds, I thank God you lost that baby. It means a fresh start, with nothing to come between us. Okay, if you want kids, we'll have kids. As many as you like. But give me at least a couple of years with you all to myself first. Then, when we do have a baby, it'll be *ours*, yours and mine, not just half you and half some no-good Italian peasant."

Flooded with acid memories, Carla's eyes brimmed with hot, stinging tears. She blinked too late to stop the flow. Jack cursed under his breath.

"Carla, I just can't handle the way you keep crying. Maybe I expressed myself crudely just then. If so, I'm truly sorry. I guess it's hard for a man to understand these things. But you can't weep forever over something that worked out for the best."

Carla dried her eyes hastily and collected her shattered wits. Her face was white.

"No, Jack," she said firmly, trying desperately to hide her anguish, "it just wouldn't work."

He finally exploded.

"I am sick to death," he roared, "of you making a tragedy out of every damn scene. Of course it'll work, if you'd give it half a chance. This past week you've been different, more relaxed, more *fun* than you've ever been. I thought you were finally letting me see the real you. That's what gave me the courage to ask you to marry me. But I just can't take all this agonising. It's getting to be a pain in the neck. The day you become my wife, Carla, this neurotic guilt-trip you're on is finally over, once and for all. Now stop making heavy weather of everything. I know perfectly well you love me, this week you finally stopped hiding it. Love's pretty scary, I admit, but love is a challenge, love I can handle. Guilt I can't. Guilt is dirty, degrading, and self-indulgent. I love you, Carla. So help me, I have never said that to a woman before."

"I believe you," said Carla, in agony now. "That's precisely why I can't marry you."

"And what kind of logic is that supposed to be?"

"It's nothing to do with logic. You just can't accept,

145

can you, that you can't have everything you want, just like that. I might as well be a company, or some stock, or a show you'd decided to back. You love me all right, but strictly on your terms. You want love with no strings, no concessions, no small print. You want the freehold, the sole franchise, the first option. You want it bright and shining with all the rust removed and a fresh coat of paint on top. Well, that's something you can't buy, arrange, or win with loaded dice. I won't marry you, Jack. I can't marry you. Please don't make me keep on saying it."

The quiet, forceful finality of this speech was like a slap in the face. Not like the impassioned, provocative slap of their first encounter, but deliberate, calculated, and insulting.

"I do believe she really means it," said Jack at last wonderingly. "She's not just playing hard to get."

"You cotton on real fast, man. She really means it."

"Don't think you can play games with me, Carla. I'm not some lovesick kid with a crush on you. I'm not going to plead, or ask you twice."

"Good," said Carla, controlling the tremor in her voice, frightened by the unfamiliar pain and anger in Jack's face.

He kept his promise. He didn't ask her twice. He didn't say another word. They walked back to the car some distance apart and drove back to the hotel in a fog of silence.

As if by unspoken arrangement, Jack left her alone that night, lying rigid and controlled on his side of the big double bed in a gross parody of the fateful night of the thunderstorm. It was a night of torment that tested Carla's resolve to the limits. Caught between the devil and the deep blue sea, she lay wakeful beside him until despair sucked her into sleep.

They set off for home early next morning. Jack was

unnaturally polite to her during the interminably tense car journey, strenuously avoiding even the slightest physical contact, which could only prove his undoing. Damn her. If she thought he was going to grovel and beg, she was crazy. If she thought he might resort to bribing her with promises he couldn't keep, she was a fool. Her head was so full of half-baked romantic notions about love that she couldn't see the wood for the trees. She wanted moonlight and roses, and dull domesticity. She wanted a brilliant career, and a houseful of screaming kids. She didn't know what the hell she wanted. Except that she didn't want him. Or she didn't want what she thought was him. She didn't want someone used to having things all his own way. She didn't want someone brash and successful who'd never had to suffer. Too bad, thought Jack grimly. If it was a case of pride versus love, he'd settle for pride. It had taken a beating, but it would survive. As for love ... well, he'd have to go cold turkey and like it.

Jack moved back into his own apartment that night. Carla had a frightening sense of amputation, of unbearable loss. She lay wakeful as the hours ticked by, battling against her desire to go to him, drop a bombshell on him, and see if he survived the blast. Once she even got as far as getting up, putting on her bathrobe, and opening the door before retiring, defeated, back to bed, now lonely and huge in its emptiness. She couldn't go through with it. She couldn't resort now to something which would be, at best, emotional blackmail. Put Jack on the spot, and he'd always rise to the challenge. Because he hated to admit when he was beaten, even when he knew he couldn't win. And he couldn't win, not this time, because it was she, Carla, who had the loaded dice, and she would rather lose him honestly than win him by cheating, or trick him into surrender.

Out of nowhere she remembered Molly, her agent,

theorising cynically about men, a subject she claimed to know all about. "Be careful," she had warned. "of the ones who tell you their life story. They always leave out the most important part." Well, that applied to women as well. But when you had lived a lie for long enough, you ended up believing it yourself. What if she had told him the truth from the start? Would he have asked her to marry him then? Surely not. He had said, with almost exaggerated emphasis, how glad he was that she did not have another man's child to blight their future together. How relieved he was that she had lost her baby.

Only she hadn't. After a bare six months in the safety of the womb, Paolo's child had tumbled, terrified, into an incubator, tiny, fragile and tough. It had, triumphantly, survived. And was now seven years old, sweet-natured, beautiful, very much loved, and living happily in Ealing.

Chapter Eight

Carla considered packing her bags and returning to England, but decided against it. To run away would solve nothing. Better to stay and work than sit brooding in Soho.

Superficially, at least, Jack made it easy for her. He could hardly have looked less like a spurned lover. He projected his usual dynamic self as far as work was concerned, avoiding any private encounters with Carla and treating her in front of the others with the same casual courtesy he afforded to all. She, following his example, gave no outward hint of her secret torment. She went on stage each day and gave a faultless performance, revealing no sign of the insomnia which destroyed her nights or the weight she carried during the day. The show went on regardless.

To the fascinated onlookers, it must have seemed like an amicable parting rather than a dramatic rift. Only Carla could see the pain behind Jack's eyes, the pain she had put there. She had accused him of never having suffered, of never having lost. Now he had finally and unexpectedly done both, and he didn't like it. It was more damaged pride, reasoned Carla, than unrequited love. He would get over it fast enough, find someone else. It was best for him. Jack liked to freewheel, and would have expected her to do likewise. She would be deluded indeed to expect a man like Jack to have room in his life for another man's child. Even a child like Francesca.

Mamma adored Francesca, of course. Faced with that tiny creature, hanging on to life so precariously, Mamma had forgotten her outrage, her hatred of its father, her contempt for its mother. And, bereaved a week later, Mamma had badly needed something to love. In any case Carla, who was horribly ill after her overdose and the premature birth, was in no fit state to be a mother. The minute scrap of humanity in the incubator had seemed no part of her for the first few hazy days. And then, just as she had begun to return to normality, just when she might have established some bond with her baby, Pappa had died in the very same hospital, before Carla's horrified eyes, and she had hurtled back into Hell. She had been no help whatsoever to her mother or Francesca. She had had what could only be described as a complete nervous breakdown.

Mrs de Luca had turned to her son Mario for advice, and he had consulted with his mentors in the seminary. By the time Carla was discharged, shell-shocked, from a nursing home for the mentally ill, Francesca was already ten weeks old. Mamma, in the throes of settling debts and selling up house, had exported the trouble-some Carla to the aunt in Scotland who would otherwise have presided over the latter stages of her pregnancy. When Carla was finally allowed to come out of exile to rejoin her family, they were firmly established in the new house in Ealing, with everyone from the milkman to the parish priest believing Francesca to be Mrs de Luca's child. So much so that Carla almost found herself believing it too. Almost, but not quite. Some primeval bond had survived their parting. The relationship between Carla and Francesca had always been, despite everything, something very secret and special. They were always one another's favourite sister.

Mrs de Luca had brought up her granddaughter admirably, as one might expect, but she retained an air of silent martyrdom that was not lost on Carla. Ever since that dreadful time, Carla had never felt close to her mother, and was painfully aware of her buried resentment. Carla became the odd one out, the black sheep, constantly put upon and unable, quite literally, to do a thing right. In the end she had escaped to Drama School in a desperate bid to keep her sanity and self-respect. Since then, the only thing she had managed to do which had won any overt approval from Mamma had been to associate with Remo. Mamma regarded Remo as heaven-sent absolution for Carla's sins. Mamma simply could not believe that even her foolish daughter would dare turn her back on such ill-deserved good fortune.

One Sunday, soon after Carla had left Drama School, she had been alone with her mother in the kitchen, rolling pasta, when Mrs de Luca had said, without any prior warning: "Listen to me, Carla. You marry Remo. He's a good boy. But you don't tell him about Francesca, okay? No-one wants a girl with another man's child."

This statement, so bald, so unexpected, so unprecedented, had echoed in Carla's ears for the rest of the day for Francesca was a taboo subject. Francesca was never discussed. Not once had Carla and her mother sat down together and talked about Francesca's future, as they should have done. Francesca was, by this time, three years old, and Carla realised with a jolt that if she did not, belatedly, make some kind of stand, she risked losing her for good.

After an exceedingly bad few nights alone in her bedsitter, Carla had caught the tube out to Ealing on a weekday morning, knowing that the girls would all be at school and Francesca at nursery, to seek a private interview with Mamma.

Where her courage came from she did not know, but, stammering slightly, she told her mother that she had never had any intention of abrogating responsibility for her daughter. She appreciated Mamma's help in bringing her up, but as far as she was concerned this had always been a temporary arrangement until she was financially able to take charge herself. As soon as she had a home to offer Francesca, she proposed to reclaim her.

Mamma had argued volubly. It would confuse the child, she said. It would blight Carla's chances of marriage. Without a man, how did she hope to provide Francesca with a home? Was she planning to move the child into her bedsitter? If she was so set on motherhood, she might at least have got herself a proper job with a regular wage. As it was, she just lived on her wits, a feckless member of a feckless profession. Carla let Mamma repeat all this several times in several different ways. She forced herself to remain calm while deepseated resentments and bitter recriminations were dredged up for a further airing. She remained, throughout, implacable. She would, she declared, from that day forward support Francesca financially even if she had to scrub floors to do it. If she married, her husband would have to accept Francesca as his own. If she did not, she would, by hook or crook, find some way of providing her with a home. As for Francesca herself, even Mamma could not deny that her affection for Carla was not in doubt. Carla would not, could not, believe that Francesca would object to living with her, and when she was old enough to understand she would, gently, tell her the truth. Finally, Carla threw down her trump card. She had discussed the whole matter, she said, with her Father Confessor at the Italian Church in Soho, and he fully endorsed her resolve to acknowledge her sacred duties towards her child. A lie, admittedly, but emphatically a white one. Mamma was forced to relent – and from then on treated Carla with grudging respect.

Carla's selling career owed nearly all its success to motivation. Despite the large demands the rest of the family made on her earnings, Carla had nonetheless salted away a tidy sum in the Building Society against the day when Francesca would join her. The matter had remained tacit between herself and Mamma. Privately, Mamma thought Carla's ambition a pipe dream, unless her daughter got herself a man, or a regular job, or both. She seriously doubted if Remo's suit would continue once he knew the truth about Carla's past, being too steeped in her own prejudices to imagine matters otherwise. As for Remo's pious old mother ... Mamma shuddered. No, as Carla grew older and wiser, she would come to appreciate that her mother had known best all along. Meanwhile, she conveniently ignored the fact that Carla's unorthodox selling exploits earned her far more than any humdrum office job would have done.

Carla, wrenching her mind from Jack, totted up the commission she had earned that summer. A staggering £5000 so far, with the prospect of a further £1500 or so if she maintained her output. She was only too well aware that she was not mortgageable, but she would have more than enough for key money on a decent rented flat, and ample security to keep up the rent during her lean patches. It still wouldn't be easy, but at least it would be honest. There was no longer any doubt in her mind about Remo. She couldn't marry Remo now. Not after Jack. Men! thought Carla, with sudden defiance. I can live without one!

But a few days later, the apple cart was upset yet again. A telegram arrived for Carla. It was from Molly, brisk and laconic as ever.

153

GEMMA STEVENS HOSPITALISED, it read. ANNA PRICE YOURS. RETURN PRONTO. MOLLY.

Trembling all over, Carla put through a phone call to London.

"Molly? I got your cable."

"Somebody up there loves you, Carla. The Stevens girl is in plaster from neck to toe. Car smash. Someone must have wished her break a leg with a vengeance." Molly cackled wheezily at her own joke.

"Gosh, poor girl. Will she be all right?"

"She'll live. Cut out the phony sympathy, lovie. This is your big break, remember? Rehearsals start next week. I could only get you the Equity minimum, of course. Get on your bike, for God's sake."

Carla knew she should have felt elated. She should have been over the moon on hearing this terrific news. At last she had a part with prospects. A part she could really get her teeth into. A part full of pain, to replace her own. She realised, with a pang, that she didn't want to go. That leaving Catalina meant finality. It meant never seeing Jack again. Despite the premature end to their affair, she still saw him every day, he was still, inextricably, part of her life. She would have had to leave soon anyway, but to go now was to face harsh reality earlier than expected, to exchange her half-loaf for no bread at all.

She couldn't face telling him in the site office, where he was subject to never-ending interruptions. She owed him some personal explanation. So she waited until after dinner, watched for him to return to his apartment, and boldly knocked on his door with a courage she did not feel.

When he opened it, the mask dropped. He looked suddenly tired, strained, almost haggard, totally unlike his usual workday persona, brimming with vitality and

154

strength.

"What is it?" he asked coolly, staring at her.

"Can I come in?" faltered Carla, immediately sensing the shock waves of hostility that he studiously jammed in public.

Jack sighed and made a sweeping sardonic bow as she crossed the threshold.

"A drink?" he asked, with rather laboured hospitality.

"No thanks. I've just come to tell you that I'll be leaving in a couple of days, just as soon as I can wind things up here."

Jack smiled sarcastically.

"Spare us the dramatic exit, Carla. It's hardly necessary. I wasn't planning to force my attentions on you. I thought you would have realised that by now."

"It's nothing to do with us. I heard from my agent today. I've got a part."

Jack didn't answer. He poured himself a slug of neat Bourbon and tossed in a couple of ice cubes. He shook it thoughtfully, the ice rattling against the crystal tumbler.

"Terrific. Suitably highbrow, I hope."

"Not exactly. It's a fringe play. I auditioned for it back in the summer and the girl who beat me to it has had to drop out. I was next in line."

"Hmm. You don't sound all that enthusiastic. Don't you rate the play?"

"Of course I'm enthusiastic, it's just such a surprise. The play is extraordinary, with the best part for a woman in ages."

"Appropriately tragic, I trust? Comedy's hardly your style."

"Please, Jack, don't snipe at me. It's not tragedy and it's not comedy either. It's real life, about people who live and love and hurt each other . . ."

155

"Just like us."

". . . and survive."

"Just like us?"

"We've no choice, have we? In a month you'll have forgotten me."

"What about you? Think you can remember me as long as that?"

"I have a very long memory."

"Too right you have. That's your whole damn trouble."

"Jack, *don't* let's start fighting again."

He tossed back his drink in one swallow.

"Want to part friends, huh?" he asked cynically.

"Why not?"

"Why *not*? Honey, take my advice. Next time you go to bed with a man, have a care. Don't give the poor sap all you've got and then leave him high and dry. He might be a whole lot meaner than me and give you what's coming to you."

"Jack, I . . ."

"I think I've sussed you out at last. You're scared to be loved, that's it, isn't it? You're scared to be obligated to anyone. You're scared to give anyone rights over you. Let me tell you, sweetheart, the knight in shining armour you've been waiting for doesn't exist because no-one can rescue you from yourself. Only you can do that. And you won't. You won't because you're so addicted to pain and guilt that you can't live without them. And you know something? Pain and guilt are kind of infectious and I sure as hell don't intend to catch them."

Jack was really angry now, the suppressed fury and disappointment triggered off by the sight of her standing there, tormenting him with her presence, her eyes huge and dark, her face pale and haunted.

Horrified at the havoc she had wrought, at the

156

strength she had undermined, Carla instinctively reached out and touched him. She couldn't bear to remember him like this, hating her. She had underestimated his capacity for hurt, for resentment. She had forced herself to imagine him shrugging her off, she could not live with the scale of her crime against him. She wanted to give comfort, to receive forgiveness.

Flinching visibly as her hand touched his arm, Jack struggled briefly, his eyes burning into hers. They just managed to whisper one another's name before their mouths met in an explosive, scorching kiss. A slow, sweet poison began to invade Carla's bloodstream. His lips, hard and demanding and angry and pleading, sucked all resistance out of her. She moaned helplessly, hopelessly. How, oh how, would she ever bear life without him?

When Jack lifted her into his arms and carried her into the bedroom, her first logical impulse should have been to retreat, to protest. But she did neither. It would be, for both of them, the last time.

Looking back, it had all seemed to happen in slow motion, a prolonged, exquisite agony searing indelibly into her memory. Jack was consumed with a savage tenderness, a desire to punish her by ensuring that never again would she reach such heights with any other man. When finally they both lay weak and expiated, he was wet with her tears. After a long, terrible silence, he said heavily, "Nothing's changed, has it?"

Carla had trouble finding her voice. When it came out it was hoarse and thick.

"Nothing's changed," she said.

"Fabulous tan, sweetie," enthused Peter Metcalfe. "Been somewhere exciting?"

"Italy, actually," Carla said, trying to ignore the lascivious glint in his eye. Automatically, she nodded acknowledgement to the other members of cast assembled in the dingy rehearsal room, smiling brightly at the two or three she recognised from previous engagements. It was rather unnerving to be the lead, knowing that other actresses in the company would all be privately thinking that they could do better.

Carla found her concentration wandering during Peter's introductory spiel. She had returned to London late the previous evening, having spent two tiring, economical days travelling by rail. Fitzgerald Enterprises had given her an air ticket, of course, but it had been worth her while to cash it in and save the difference. With typical efficiency, the commission owed to her had been wired to her bank on the day of her departure. £5745. More money than she had ever possessed in her life. Far from inducing extravagance, it had spurred her towards more stringent savings. She had still, in conscience, to buy a piano for Silvana which would make a sizeable hole in her fortune. It never occurred to her to back out of this self-inflicted commitment. To Carla's logical way of thinking, Silvana would have had a decent piano long ago if Pappa had lived and Francesca had not been born, so it was now Carla's duty to redress the balance.

She had not yet had time to see her family, and with only two weeks allocated for rehearsal, to keep down costs, she would have difficulty in fitting in all but the briefest visit. She had phoned Mamma, of course, to announce her return.

She had seemed strangely put out that Carla should have arrived home ahead of schedule, and, surprisingly, did not seem in any hurry to see her or issue the usual demands for cash. Too tired, too full of anguish to give the matter much thought, Carla had simply said that she would drop over for a few hours the following weekend, and then asked to speak to Francesca. There had

158

followed a flood of excited prattle from her daughter, and for the first time in days, Carla had actually laughed.

". . . no doubt about it," Peter Metcalfe was saying, "that, subject to backing, I've got the highest hopes that this production will move on. Freeman's earlier work was too experimental for mass audiences. This time, with a bold approach, I think we can make his ideas hit home to critics and public alike. Now, those of you who've played in Brecht will know . . ."

Carla came to with a jolt. Forget Jack, she told herself. Forget Jack, but remember what you felt. This play is all about passion.

For the next few days, Carla lived in a state of permanent fatigue, working herself to a standstill during the day and dreaming about the part all night. The dreams were a disjointed, surrealistic re-enactment of the day. She, Carla, *was* Anna Price, endlessly reliving in her sleep her tortured relationship with both husband and lover. The husband was played by Jack – strong, domineering, powerful, angry. Disconcertingly, however, Jack played the lover too – sensitive, dependent, and vulnerable. Not like the real Jack at all.

These nocturnal rehearsals left her emotionally confused and exhausted, but the resulting ravaged pallor only enhanced her credibility as Freeman's tormented heroine. The climax of the play, where she died at the hands of her jealous husband in a hideous demonstration of his selfish love for her, left Carla shattered and the rest of the cast stunned into silence. The power of the writing was beyond doubt, but Carla's portrayal gave it an added dimension. Word began to leak out, gossip began to spread. This new Freeman play was one to watch.

"Don't overdo it, Carla, sweetie," soothed Peter Metcalfe after rehearsals one evening. "Living the part is okay, but you're beginning to look ill. Let's go out to

159

dinner and unwind a bit."

"Thanks, Peter, but I'm honestly too tired to enjoy a meal. I'll have something on toast and fall into bed. It's Sunday tomorrow. I'll have a lie-in and then go to visit my mother. She'll feed me up, never fear."

"One day next week, then," he persisted.

Carla shook her head. "I'm lousy company at the moment," she apologised. "After we open, perhaps."

"You're on. Relax, Carla. You're going to be dynamite."

When she got back to Soho, she was fumbling in her bag for her key to the side door when Mrs Palucchi, spying her through the restaurant window, came scurrying out.

"Carla, Remo come for you. I let him into your room, okay?" Mrs Palucchi grinned toothily, winked conspiratorially, and disappeared back into the restaurant. Carla sighed. At least she'd had some warning.

"Remo!" she exclaimed warmly, seeing the disconsolate figure rise from the chair as she entered. "Why didn't you ring first? Have you been waiting long? You know how it is with rehearsals." She kissed him briefly on each cheek. "I was going to pop in to see you tomorrow," she continued brightly, gabbling slightly, taking off her coat and hanging it up. "Didn't Mamma tell you I'd be coming? Coffee?"

Remo smiled rather stiffly.

"No coffee, thank you. Yes, she told me. She asked me to come here tonight."

Carla hesitated, puzzled.

"Why? Is something wrong? I spoke to her a few days ago, she didn't mention anything . . ."

"Sit down, Carla," said Remo awkwardly. "It will take a few minutes to explain."

"Explain *what*?" burst out Carla, suddenly alarmed. She was tired, her nerves stretched to breaking point.

What had Mamma and Remo been cooking up now?

"Relax," said Remo quietly. "Nobody's ill, nothing like that."

Carla crossed quickly to the bed and sat down, her mind whirring. Mamma had been somewhat stilted on the phone, come to think of it. She should have picked up that something was brewing.

"Carla, while you were away, your mother came to see me with a problem," began Remo slowly.

"Money," said Carla immediately, her conditioned reflexes heightened by an uneasy sense of premonition.

"Money. The repayments on the house, to be precise."

"Repayments? But the house is already paid for!" interrupted Carla. "That's why she bought it in the first place. It was cheap enough to buy outright because she couldn't have got a mortgage –"

"That's right," acknowledged Remo steadily. "But the deeds to a house are good security. She's been raising money on them, over a number of years, with a finance company. She didn't like to tell you because she thought you'd make a scene."

"But there was no *need* for Mamma to borrow money!" exploded Carla. "Everything I give her is on top of her Social Security. If they had any idea of how much I give her, she'd probably be prosecuted or something! All the girls are well provided for. Apart from what I've saved for – for a rainy day – I've given her every penny I've earned. *Why*?"

"Carla, try to understand. You mother's a good woman, but she spends money like your Pappa was still alive. She can't help it. She's not used to economising, she has no savings to fall back on. She doesn't like to feel poor. So, she thought she would borrow, just a little at first. Then she borrowed a bit more. And then a bit more. For a long time now, Carla, most of your

161

money has been going to pay the interest on the loan."

Carla sat speechless. Francesca's clothes, Silvana's music lessons, Angela's school trips, all the things she thought she had paid for had been bought with borrowed money.

"Then, while you were away in Italy, it all caught up with her. She'd already missed several repayments, spent the money you'd given her before she could bank it. Those finance companies don't mess about. They threatened to foreclose the loan."

"Oh God," muttered Carla.

"Which would have meant her losing the house and no end of disgrace in front of the neighbours. She was beside herself. You know how proud your mother is, how respectable."

"But *why* didn't she tell me?" demanded Carla. "Why didn't she write to me? I could have talked to my boss, sent an advance on my commission. I could have—"

"She didn't tell you, Carla, because she felt guilty. She decided to come to me instead."

"Guilty?" Carla laughed mirthlessly. "You're saying that *she* felt guilty?"

"Besides," continued Remo stolidly, "you couldn't have helped. The loan company were fed up with her broken promises. They wanted immediate repayment. In full."

There was a deathly pause.

"How much?" whispered Carla, her mind flying to her precious nest-egg, her throat dry.

Remo didn't answer immediately.

"A lot," he said at last. "But don't worry. I paid it."

Horrified, Carla began to put two and two together. Her arithmetic was shaky from shock.

"*You* paid it? *You paid it*? And who's going to pay you?"

162

"I don't want paying back."

Carla stood up, and started pacing the tiny room.

"I just don't believe it!" she stormed. "I *can't* believe
it. Oh, I'm miles ahead of you, never fear. This is money
at the altar of the great god Family. A sort of dowry
in reverse. You're practically her son, right? How dare
she put you in this position! How dare she compromise
me like this!"

"Carla, calm down. It's not what you think –"

"Get this straight, Remo!" Carla was dizzy with rage.
"I appreciate your trying to help and I'll pay you back
somehow, every penny. But you can tell Mamma from
me to put this in her pipe and smoke it. She's not taking
out any loans on *me*! I refuse to be her collateral! Before
she sold me off to you, Remo, just how much did she
bother to tell you first?"

"Carla, if only you'd let me –"

"Did you look at the small print first, Remo? Or did
she make sure you didn't see it? Did she tell you about
the unexpected bonus of marriage to me? The small
matter of my little –"

"*Carla!*" interrupted Remo, exasperated. "For God's
sake, you've got it all wrong. I'm going to marry
Gabriella!"

Carla sat down on the bed, the sudden silence of the
room humming all around her.

"Gabriella?" she repeatedly blankly.

"You're not upset, are you, Carla? Your mother and
Gabby were worried you'd be upset. But of course, I
knew that you didn't –"

"No, no," she muttered, stunned and relieved.

A huge weight seemed to have been lifted from
Remo's long-suffering shoulders.

"I know what you're thinking," he continued self-
mockingly. "What does an ardent feminist like Gabby
want with an old stick-in-the-mud like me? I've asked

163

her the same question myself, but she just laughs."

"Oh Remo," said Carla with a pang of conscience, "don't say that. Gabby was always the brightest of all of us. She knows a good man when she sees one."

Lost for words, she put her arms around him and gave him a long, affectionate hug.

"I was giving her a lift up to Maxwell's each day," reminisced Remo, his face lighting up, "and then we started meeting occasionally for lunch. And it all went on from there. Your Mamma's troubles sort of threw us together, accelerated everything, brought everything out in the open. It's all so ironic, isn't it?

"Gabby's a bit like you, you know, Carla. All independent and self-sufficient on the outside, and all soft and frightened underneath. I had an awful job convincing her that you had packed me in. And even after I convinced her, I had problems. She had some dreadful hang-up about you and me that you wouldn't let me in on. Eventually, I hope you'll forgive me, I wrung it all out of her, and then I understood. She's so terribly fond of you, Carla. And of Francesca. She felt that she was robbing both your futures. Your Mamma's always been so fixated on you and me getting married, and only poor Gabby knew the reason why. I admire you, Carla, more than I can say, for how honest you were with me. Any other girl would have used me as a meal ticket."

"Oh, Remo," sobbed Carla, all the agony spilling out of her. "Honest is the last thing I am. Oh, why do I have to cause everybody so much pain?" Too tired and drained to keep up a front any longer, she wept shamelessly on his shoulder while he rocked her to and fro like a small child.

"Listen, Carla," he said. "Gabby and I have talked a lot about all this. You and Francesca will always have a home with us, we want you to know that. I'm buying a house, a big one, but we won't be living in it till Gabby graduates next year. Why don't you and Francesca move in meanwhile? Your mother can babysit while you work. It will be a start, a chance to begin a new life together.

"Carla, darling, you've got to tell Francesca the truth. You mustn't leave it too late. I've talked to your mother, I know the whole story. My poor, poor Carla, how you must have suffered. Don't cry, carissima. Everything's going to be all right."

His words seemed to give her no comfort, rather the reverse. He was astonished at the extent of Carla's weeping. He had never, till today, ever seen her cry. Huge spasms of pain wracked her. Tears like this were for death, disaster. They seemed excessive, unhealthy.

"Carla, Carla," he expostulated gently. "Dry your eyes. There's no harm done."

She looked up at him, her face disfigured in its raw agony.

"Tell me, Carla," urged Remo, seeing a story in her eyes that he did not yet know. "Tell me what it is."

So Carla told him.

Telling him took a long time as Carla's narrative was haphazard and fragmented, not to say suitably censored, but Remo read between the lines sufficiently to realise that Carla's love affair with Jack Fitzgerald had been akin to the bursting of a dam, the resulting flood leaving wholesale devastation in its wake.

She had done the right thing in breaking it off, Carla protested between sobs. The relationship was pure chemistry; in every other way they were grossly unsuited to one another. Jack was dynamic, restless and rootless. He liked excitement, mobility, variety. He hated ties, permanency, restrictions.

"Jack lives from day to day," gulped Carla. "He sees what he wants, goes after it, and moves on. He dominates everything and everybody. His life's sort of ... effortless, always on his terms. He wanted a playmate, not a wife. And certainly not a child. Let alone another man's."

"But shouldn't you at least have given him a chance?" remonstrated Remo mildly. "How can you judge him when he didn't know the truth? Besides, a man's got a right to know just why he's been turned down." There was a rueful edge to his voice.

"I did tell him why I was turning him down. I just didn't explain about Francesca. There was no point in dragging her into it, after all."

"Dragging her into it? You deliberately left her out. That was wrong of you. Has it occurred to you that you might have underestimated him? Men feel just as deeply as women, you know, they're just conditioned not to show it. Do you think *I* would have minded? Do you think it would make any difference to Gabby and me now if Francesca were hers and not yours?"

Carla shook her head. "You're not Jack," she said stubbornly. "You're a natural family man, and you're soft-hearted to a fault. Oh, Jack would have taken Francesca on board, no doubt, if that was the price of marriage. When Jack wants something, he pays up and looks cheerful. He'd have been generous, too, with material things – clothes, schooling, and so on. But he wouldn't have had any room for her in his mind, or in his heart. She would just have been part of the contract, that's all. And sooner or later, when the passion wore off, and we found we had nothing in common, Francesca would have been the scapegoat.

"Jack's all action, money, success. Superficial things. I need a strong man, I realise that, but one who's got depth, one who understands about feelings, not one who's on a whistle-stop tour of life. To Jack, feelings are just sensations, life's purely for kicks. All his millions

166

won't buy the kind of security I need for Francesca. He told me once that he was all 'up front', honest, frank, a bit shallow. He's never pretended to be something he's not. That's why I'm so sure I did the right thing. But it hurts, Remo. It hurts."

Holding the weeping Carla in his arms, Remo could feel the hurt vibrating through her. Damn Jack Fitzgerald, he fumed, out of loyalty and affection for Carla. Damn all brash American playboy tycoons. He sighed.

"If you're quite sure, as you say, that you did the right thing," he said firmly, "then you must learn to forget him. Listen to me, Carla. Tomorrow Gabby and I will take you to see the house. Tomorrow you will tell Francesca who she is. And a week from now you will give that part of yours everything you've got. You owe it to yourself and Francesca to make it a success."

"I owe it to the play," mumbled Carla at last. "Without the play I'd have gone to pieces."

Chapter Nine

After nearly three months away, Carla's homecoming visit was something of an occasion with even the moody Angela jostling for her share of the hugs and kisses. Silvana, whose piano had been delivered the previous day, was still quite overcome. Gabby, reassured repeatedly by Remo that Carla was not upset, was bubbling like a schoolgirl, displaying a large diamond. Francesca, with all the confidence of the established favourite, held back good-naturedly while the others monopolised Carla before running forward to claim her share of the attention. Mrs de Luca was oddly subdued, to the point of sheepishness, although this was discernible only to Carla and Gabby as Mamma presided over Sunday lunch in her usual matriarchal fashion, quizzing her eldest daughter sternly about the weather, food and prices in Tuscany, and grunting her disapproval of the latter in particular, and her mistrust of Northerners in general. Angela and Silvana were then briskly directed towards the washing up, under Mamma's supervision, while Francesca was allowed to accompany Carla, Remo and Gabby on the excursion to the new house.

Carla, sitting in the back of the car with her daughter, wondered how on earth she would set about breaking the news to her. Francesca, enjoying the luxury of having Carla at home, was at her most appealing, which didn't make the task ahead one jot easier. Remo explained as he drove that the house had come on to the market some time ago, and that he had already been negotiating for it before he and Gabby had made their plans. He had been looking for some months now for a house large enough to accommodate a self-contained flat for his mother. He circumlocuted the reason for this with admirable loyalty and tact, but plainly Remo's intent had been to distance his carping mother from his private life without condemning her to a lonely old age.

The house was a large Edwardian semi with both a basement and an upper floor, formerly converted into four rented flats and now being sold with rather dilapidated vacant possession.

"Don't you see?" Gabby took over excitedly. "Remo's mother will have the basement, we'll have the ground and first floors, and the top flat will eventually be—" she blushed "—for an au pair, nanny, or whatever. But in the meantime, there's absolutely no reason why you and—why you can't move in."

"As long as you don't mind the noise of the workmen," added Remo.

"And of course you would save the rent on your bedsit..."

"...because we wouldn't expect you to pay anything, seeing as it would otherwise be empty."

Interrupting each other in their well-meaning eagerness, their sincerity was touchingly beyond question. Carla, seizing the moment, looked down at Francesca.

"Well?" she asked jauntily. "Would you like to come and live with me in Remo and Gabby's house? To keep me company?"

Francesca's eyes opened wide.

"Would I have my own room?" she asked disbelievingly. "Instead of sharing with Silvana?"

"Oh, definitely," confirmed Remo. "There are any number of rooms. And you can still go to the same school, because it's not far from where you live now."

"And my own wardrobe for my clothes?" pursued Francesca, practically. "And can I be first in the bath?"

Gabby snorted in amusement. The pecking order at bathtime decreed that poor Francesca always got Silvana's bathwater, after Angela had had first dip. Although Francesca had never questioned the traditional justice of these arrangements, she had clearly been nurturing extravagant dreams beyond her station.

"Of course," put in Gabby, trying to keep a straight face. "Unless, of course, you prefer to have a shower."

"A *shower*?" gasped Francesca. This was an as yet unsampled treat. "Oh, yes please! But will Mamma let me come?" she added dubiously.

Carla held her breath while she said a quick prayer, and plunged in headlong.

"What would you say," she asked levelly, "if I told you that Mamma is really your Mamma's Mamma?"

Remo and Gabby, unprepared, exchanged glances and then looked stolidly ahead. Francesca, in her typical calm fashion, appeared to be giving the question some thought. She looked at Carla with those huge brown eyes, her candid, childish trusting gaze demanding nothing less that the whole truth.

"You see, Francesca darling," Carla heard herself saying, "*I'm* your real mother. That's why I've always loved you best. When you were born I was too young to take care of you. But now, if you want to, I'd very much like to have you live with me. Of course, if you prefer to stay with your *Nona*, that's all right. I would be disappointed, but I would understand."

Francesca was very quiet. Oh hell, thought Carla miserably, what a mess I made of that. One didn't confront a small child with a bombshell in so forthright a fashion.

171

She should have made a little story out of it, explained slowly, patiently, carefully. Any self-respecting social worker would have been duly horrified at her straight-forward clumsiness.

"Does that mean," asked Francesca, after an age, "that Angela is my *auntie*?"

Carla, despite her trepidation, found her lips twitching in amusement at the comic disgust in Francesca's voice.

"I'm afraid so," she nodded. "And Gabby and Silvana, too."

"Oh, I don't mind about *them*," said Francesca crossly, "but Angela is bossy enough already. Once she's my aunt, she'll be impossible!"

And suddenly they were all laughing, and Francesca was squeezing Carla's hand tightly.

"I didn't mean it," she said reassuringly, "about the bath. I really don't mind if you go first."

Adults always underestimated, thought Carla, the immense adaptability of children. All this would be far, far harder for poor Mamma than it would be for Francesca who was soon scampering, quite carefree, all over the new house which was full of doors and landings and hidey-holes. She particularly loved its wild, unkempt garden, complete with ancient apple tree and murky ornamental pond. The top floor flat, Remo explained, would be given a quick coat of paint to enable Carla to move in as soon as possible after completion. He and Gabby were expecting to sign contracts any day, and then renovations would begin almost immediately.

"A lot of banging and crashing about, I'm afraid," said Gabby, "but once they've completed the bottom part of the house, you could move into that while they do the rest. Luckily, we don't need a new roof. The old landlord got one of those Council grants."

It was fascinating to see the self-sufficient and ambitious Gabriella so caught up with domestic matters, although her brightness and vivacity were stronger than ever under the new stimulus. Old Mrs Panetta, thought Carla wryly, would shortly find she'd met her match.

While Carla was busy telling the truth to Francesca, Mrs de Luca was preparing her two youngest daughters for a similar shock.

"Your sister," intoned Mamma, "was young and foolish. She met a bad man. Let it be a lesson to both of you. But we must thank God that he gave us a good child like Francesca. Now it's time for Carla to do her duty."

"Can I tell them at school," pressed the status-conscious Angela, "that I've got a niece?"

Mrs de Luca bristled at the delayed-action gossip that was now unavoidable.

"You better ask Carla," she stated briskly. "Now get on with your homework."

The secret of Francesca's parentage proved to be a nine-day wonder, and after the initial flurry of knowing remarks the dust died down surprisingly quickly. Mercifully, Francesca displayed no curiosity about her father, largely because she had been used from birth to the idea of not having one and had only the most childish notions of what paternity actually involved. That bridge would have to be crossed eventually, when she started asking questions. In the meantime, Carla reminded herself, she ought to marry someone who would fill the gap in Francesca's life, give her the kind of father she deserved. Someone like Remo, not someone like Jack. But not yet. Not yet.

Carla gave Mrs Palucchi a month's notice on her bed-sitter with the minimum of explanation. She didn't relish the idea of becoming an object of speculation in Soho as well as in Ealing, and had decided that it would be best to keep her private life quite separate from her professional one. One of the advantages of living out in the suburbs would be that it would be easier to compartmentalise acting and motherhood.

"Streetwise", like Freeman's two earlier plays, was due to open at the Gallery, an unprepossessing converted warehouse in Camden Town, so called because the only way to accommodate the audience in the space available was by means of steeply tiered benches overlooking the central acting area. The spectators were literally breathing down the players' necks, the lighting and props were basic to the point of non-existence, and exits and entrances had to be made through the auditorium via the four aisles which divided the seating into segments. The Gallery was a theatre club, for economic and legal reasons, and habitually only the most dedicated of theatre buffs bothered to make the journey to Camden in order to sit in discomfort for two and a half hours watching obscure plays by largely unknown writers. The Gallery had never yet spawned a West End transfer, and until now had taken a stubborn pride in its negative track record. All very well while it retained its Arts Council grant (which expired next year) and GLC funding (due to run out even sooner). Only subsidy had enabled it to eke out its meagre existence from one obscure production to the next. But now, not to put too fine a point on it, the Gallery was desperately short of cash and badly needed a good, old-fashioned, seat-filling hit.

Carla, along with everyone else, was sorely disappointed in Josiah Freeman himself. He had been prevailed upon to put in a nominal appearance at rehearsal, because the cast rather expected it, but he obstinately refused to discuss the most minor rewrites and passed no enlightening comments whatsoever as to the play's intentions. Middle-aged, rather portly, and bespect-

174

acled, he was entirely lacking in any social graces. After his obviously reluctant visit, he was not seen again, clearly indifferent as to whether his play was a success or not. One could only marvel that so much spirit and creativity lurked behind the cold-fish exterior. As far as Peter Metcalfe was concerned, however, Freeman's non-participation was a definite plus factor. He had long been of the opinion that playwrights were a confounded nuisance, and a thorn in the flesh of all self-respecting directors. Too bad they couldn't all be hermits like Freeman, or better still dead like Shakespeare. He was already thinking ahead to his plans to stage a modern-dress version of Macbeth, set in strife-torn Latin America.

At Carla's specific request, none of her family was to attend the first night. It wasn't at all a suitable play for the younger girls, Mamma would have disapproved of its morals, and she didn't want Remo and Gabby in the audience until her nerves had settled later in the week.

Gratifyingly, tickets were selling well. Peter had a lot of contacts, and had successfully generated a great deal of curiosity about the play with the result that a surprising number of critics were due to attend, although the Gallery didn't usually rate Fleet Street reviews. This made Carla even more apprehensive than usual. Her secret battle against stage-fright wrought havoc with her digestion. For two whole days before opening night, she was unable to keep any food down at all, and was forced, repeatedly, to remember that fateful night when Jack had held her head over an Italian washbasin. Nothing helped, not even yoga. But she knew from experience that after one successful performance, her confidence would return and she would start to feel human again.

By the time the house lights were dimmed on the

play's first night, Carla, waiting to go on, was in a trance of pure terror. Then, like a true professional, she responded automatically to her cue and from that moment forgot Carla de Luca and the audience, for in Anna Price's mind neither existed. It was something of a shock to return to her true self after Act One. Rather than embrace tea and reality, she kept herself in suspended animation, speaking to no-one in the interval and locking herself in the lavatory, afraid of overhearing any stray comments, favourable or otherwise, which might affect her concentration. It was only after it was all over, only after the cheers and the applause, the hugs and congratulations, that she put on her old identity like a discarded cloak to learn, belatedly, that she had caused a sensation.

"Have you seen the papers yet?" yelled Gabby down the phone next morning. "Have you seen the *Daily News*?"

Carla, after her first good night in weeks, was still groggy.

"Not yet," she admitted, yawning.

". . . 'a brilliant new playwright and an astonishing – *astonishing* – young actress conspired together to make this my most memorable evening in the theatre this year. It is devoutly to be wished that "Streetwise" reaches the larger audience it so richly deserves.' Oh Carla! This is it! Aren't you excited?"

"Er, yes – I suppose so," Carla agreed weakly.

"Just wait till all Mamma's cousins come to see you," teased Gabby. "Do you think London's got a theatre large enough?"

Carla laughed, groaned, staggered back to bed, buried her face in the pillow and slept for the rest of the morning.

What Gabby, in her naiveté, did not realise, was that

one of the dangers of a possible transfer was that a well-known actress with box-office pulling power would be brought in to take over the lead. Carla didn't like to disillusion her sister in her joyful assumption that Carla was all set for a West End triumph. It took more than critical acclaim to attract hard-nosed backers, and often money was only forthcoming with a few cast-iron guarantees like a famous name in lights to attract the crowds. Peter Metcalfe, together with Simon Duff, the earnest General Manager of the Gallery, spent a great deal of time engaged in ardent salesmanship without any obvious results. Ben Holmes would not have short-listed either of them.

Despite the rave reviews and full houses every night, the play's future remained uncertain. It gradually became clear that there was no queue of established actresses hustling for Carla's rôle. There was a real danger, in this case, of receiving unfavourable comparison with the part's creator, a risk that no-one seemed particularly keen to take. Ironically, this did not help the play, as an approach from a well-known leading lady would probably have secured its survival. Miserably, Carla felt that in some measure this was her fault, although she was too modest to voice the reason why. The cast were routinely sounded out and confirmed, predictably, that they were all prepared to transfer if the chance arose on minimum wages to reduce the level of finance required. The alternative, for most of them, would in any case have been to 'rest'.

Fortunately, Carla's mind was too absorbed in her plans for Francesca to take these problems home with her at night. She hoped for a success in order to build security for herself and her daughter, but deep down she did not expect it. Her career had had false starts before, although not on this scale. It was safer to take each day as it came and remain healthily sceptical.

Eventually, Carla could no longer postpone accepting Peter Melcalfe's insistent invitations, and decided that it would be better to get their long-delayed dinner date out of the way before she moved into Remo's house. He had arranged to pick her up at the theatre one Saturday night, half an hour after curtain. Carla had no private dressing room, of course, sharing the cramped facilities available with three other actresses. After bidding her colleagues good night, she sat idly waiting for him to arrive, filing her nails abstractedly, her thoughts far away from dinner with Peter. Professionally, she had a lot of time for him. Personally, she wished heartily that she had never, all those months ago, led him on so cold-bloodedly. That behaviour was worthy of the old, conniving Carla, not the present battered but more honest edition.

Hearing a tap on the door, she buttoned her blouse hastily to make herself respectable and called, "It's okay, Peter, you can come in," as she peered in the mirror to tidy her hair.

Her comb froze in mid-air as she saw the achingly familiar reflection in the glass, a ghost come back to haunt her.

"Sorry to disappoint you," said Jack dryly.

Carla swallowed hard.

"H-hello, Jack," she said brightly. "How lovely to see you. Did you enjoy the play?"

He sat down and stretched out his long legs.

"A bit heavyweight for my simple tastes, as you'd expect," he said, eyeing her with a candour that brought the colour to her cheeks. "But congratulations anyway. You carried the whole show." The compliment was guarded.

"Well, that's very sweet of you, Jack, but then it's the sort of chance every actress dreams about. You really can't go wrong with a part like that."

Aware that she sounded like a twittering idiot, Carla allowed an awkward silence to fall. Awkward for her, that is. Jack himself was relaxed to the point of belligerence.

"How's Ben?" she asked at last. She had nearly said, 'How's Helen?' biting her tongue just in time.

"Contemplating a second stab at holy wedlock. My fault for suggesting a cruise. Let's hope he strikes luckier second time around. How's Peter?"

"Peter? Oh, Peter! Well, actually..." But at that point, mercifully, Peter Metcalfe walked in through the open door and, not noticing Jack, gave Carla a smacking theatrical kiss.

"Hurry up, you gorgeous creature," he urged her. "I'm absolutely ravenous."

"Er, Peter," mumbled Carla, seeing Jack's lip curl in malicious amusement, "may I introduce Jack —"

"Fitz*gerald*!" exclaimed Peter, grasping Jack by the hand and pumping it energetically. "And where have you been hiding yourself? I rang your office only the other day and they said you were out of town."

"You know me, Pete," smiled Jack lazily. "I get around."

"Well, you're just the man I want to talk to," continued Peter ingratiatingly. "I don't need to tell you why. If you saw the play tonight, you'll be several jumps ahead of me already. Why not join Carla and me for dinner? This little lady," he announced, slapping Carla's rump in familiar fashion, "is the hottest property in town."

"In *Camden* Town, perhaps," modified Carla, horribly embarrassed at Peter's fulsome manner and the cynical glint in Jack's eye.

"Carla, sweetie, let's drop the false modesty for once. You may not realise it, but Jack is a man who can spot a box-office success from the other side of the Atlantic.

Isn't that right, Jack? I say, do you two know each other?"

"We don't," put in Jack before Carla could speak. "I just took the liberty of coming backstage to offer my congratulations."

Carla fell silent with relief. If Peter got the slightest idea of her relationship with Jack, he would no doubt put her under intolerable pressure to exploit it in order to help the play. Jack, instinctively, had protected her, and the shaft of gratitude was like a sharp pain.

They went to a Greek restaurant within walking distance, regularly patronised by Gallery audiences. Carla said little during the meal, fiddling with her food while Jack ate steadily, throwing her an occasional satirical glance while Peter, gesturing wildly with his fork, let every dish grow cold.

Peter didn't bother to be subtle. He knew that Jack had money, plenty of it, and backed only commercial winners so he concentrated all his energy into convincing Jack that "Streetwise" was the biggest potential hit since "The Sound of Music". He rather overdid it, Carla thought, cringing.

Jack was clearly enjoying himself, baiting Peter mercilessly with trick questions. Carla was reminded uncomfortably of their first meeting when she had devoted several hours to trying to sell him one of his own apartments. His perception and criticisms of the play were surprisingly acute, although he suggested various ways of 'tightening it up' which would, in her opinion, have destroyed its balance. But it was hard to work out which of his remarks were serious and which merely provocative.

Carla had no stomach for this type of bargaining. It offended her to see Peter practically grovelling at Jack's feet. Peter was no salesman, he was pitching it all wrong. Not that Peter saw himself as a salesman, of course.

They were a breed beneath his contempt.

"If you two gentlemen don't mind," she said eventually, stifling a convincing yawn, "I'll just hop into a taxi and take myself off home. I'm absolutely dead, and I'm sure you two still have lots to talk about."

"No need for a cab," said Jack languidly. "My car's parked close by. Which way are you headed?"

"Soho," muttered Carla, cornered, thankful she hadn't yet moved to Ealing.

"I'm staying at the Sheraton," Jack continued casually. "It'll be no trouble to drop you off. I'm pretty tired myself, if you'll forgive me, Pete. Can I offer you a lift somewhere?"

"Oh . . . er, I've got my own car, thanks," said Peter, quickly sizing up the situation. "I suppose it is rather late. If you want to go and fetch your car, Jack, Carla can meet you outside. You won't mind, will you, if I have a few words with her first while I'm waiting for the bill? Shop, you know." He stood up and shook Jack's hand vigorously. "How long are you going to be in London, Jack?" he asked anxiously.

"Who knows?" Jack said with a malevolent smile. "Here today, gone tomorrow, that's me."

"Well, perhaps you'd think over what we talked about tonight," continued Peter, disappointed. "Whoever takes this play on stands to make a lot of money."

"Message received and understood," said Jack firmly. "See you in a few minutes, Carla. So long, Pete. Take it easy."

"Carla!" Peter hissed as soon as he had gone. "This bloke's practically our last hope."

"So?" she demanded, dreading what was coming next.

"Well, there's no harm in encouraging him a tiny bit, is there? I mean, I'm not suggesting, of course, that you—"

181

"No, Peter," she said tersely.

"For God's sake, Carla, use your loaf! Surely there's no harm in stringing him along a little? I noticed the way he was looking at you, even if you didn't. I mean, what harm would it do? Think of the play, your career, the company . . ."

"Good night, Peter," Carla said, controlling herself with difficulty, aware that he was only asking her to play a more advanced version of the game she had, to her shame, played with him. "If you'll excuse me, I must go to the powder room. Good night."

Safely locked in the Ladies, Carla took a few deep breaths. It was no good. She was shaking from head to foot. Distasteful though she had found Peter's haggling, obscene though she found his crass suggestions, she felt obscurely disappointed that Jack had shown no inclination to back the play, if only for *her* sake.

It was quite unreasonable of her, of course, given the terms on which they had parted. It was irrational to expect the likes of Jack to invest money for sentimental reasons, against his own financial judgment. It was only to be expected that an impassioned, unfashionable play like "Streetwise" would have little personal appeal for a man who took life as it came and despised those who agonised over it. But what, exactly, did Jack want? Had he really sought her out just to congratulate her? Or was he on the loose in London, looking up an old flame to brighten up his stay? That sounded uncomfortably like Jack's style. Easy come, easy go.

Jack was waiting outside the restaurant in his black BMW. He didn't bother to ask for directions, because it soon became plain that he wasn't heading for Soho.

"This isn't the right way, Jack," she began. "If you turn right at the next lights . . ." But Jack just kept going.

"Where are you taking me?" asked Carla frostily, rapidly losing her battle to remain nonchalant and not

182

to over-react.

"To my hotel, of course. I want to have a talk, some-where private and civilised, without Metcalfe breathing down our necks or landladies listening through the wall."

"Talk? What about?"

"What do you think? About some unfinished business, of course."

"If you're after a one-night stand for old time's sake there's nothing doing."

"What a suspicious, sordid little mind you have. But come to think of it, that wouldn't be a bad idea, except that I didn't think to hide all the ashtrays first." And before she could come up with a suitable retort, Jack was handing his car keys to a commissionaire and whisking her skywards towards his suite.

Carla sat down gingerly on a white settee and numbly accepted the drink Jack poured her.

"Jack, it's very late . . ." she began.

"I wanted to explain to you, in private," he said, "that even though I thought you gave a superb performance tonight, I'm not going to back the play. I never had any intention of backing it, and nothing Metcalfe said tonight has made me change my mind. I don't, however, want you to think that I'm withholding my money just to get even with you for ditching me. I'm not the type of guy to bear a grudge, it's a matter of principle, that's all. I won't have you taking it personally. Knowing you, I figured you probably would."

Typical Jack. Blunt. Forthright. Insensitive.

"Leave me out of it," she said. "You're making a big mistake, that's all. It's a pity someone with your financial muscle can't see a work of art when it's staring him in the face. But then, I wouldn't expect you to."

"Uh-huh. A regular hick, that's me. But at least I don't talk a load of pretentious horseshit like lover-boy

183

Metcalfe."

"What do you mean, 'lover-boy Metcalfe'?"

"Don't act dumb. That guy's got the hots for you and you know it. Sorry if I spoilt your evening. I guess three was a crowd."

"Peter happens to be a very sincere and genuine person. My relationship with him is nothing whatsoever to do with you."

"Just glad to see you've finally got rid of all your old hang-ups about men, Carla, honey. And there's nothing like mixing business with pleasure for a busy working actress. Still, you might be wise to keep him on short rations for a while. Good insurance until you're sure he won't sell you down the river. You're still an unknown, remember?"

"After that barrage of insults," Carla cut in, embracing anger to avoid pain, "I'm forced to believe that you do bear a grudge after all."

Jack paused. "Could be you're right at that. Maybe I've been kidding myself."

He crossed over to where she sat, her head thrown back and her eyes defiant, and put his hands on her shoulders. It was the first time he had touched her since their last night and the old attraction still took her breath away. There was a tingling feeling down her spine, a distinct shortage of breath, a rush of blood to the head.

"You still feel it too, don't you?" he asked unnecessarily, her perceptible trembling telling him all he needed to know. "Why in hell are we fighting this, Carla? Why?"

I could tell him now, she thought dizzily, her reason sapped by the touch of his hands. She could have Jack and Francesca, too.

"Jack –" she began hesitantly.

"Yes?" He sat down on the couch beside her and kissed her hair, her neck. She inhaled his presence with all the fervour of a long-deprived addict, agonised to realise that she would not be able to resist him, that she was seconds away from total surrender, pathetic in her weakness, wretched in her cowardice. She couldn't bear, she simply couldn't bear, any more pain. She had come full circle, physical desire blotting out all logic, all responsibility, all common sense. Let him make love to you, a little voice said. Then tell him about Francesca. Then live happily ever after. Until . . .

Her mind raced to her daughter, trusting, innocent, accepting her new mother without reproach for the years of neglect, years that still had to be made up for. Francesca needing a father, a real father. Francesca playing second fiddle to a man so demanding that he would regard her as so much excess baggage, an unavoidable tax on love. Surely that was no way to repay her for her unquestioning loyalty to a mother who had already abused her. Suddenly, vividly, she saw Francesca dumped back with Mamma while she and Jack roamed the world and burned out their selfish passion. Oh where would she find the strength to resist him? Once she gave in, she would be totally lost. She had no more will to fight. She could feel his breath on her cheek, his hands on her breasts.

"Carla," he whispered. "I can't live without you. Please, Carla." His lips hovered over hers, teasing, tantalising, tormenting, waiting for a response, a sign, a message. With only seconds to decide, she escaped the only way she knew how. By attacking his pride.

"Jack," she said steadily, hating herself, "if I sleep with you, will you back the play?"

There was a truly dreadful silence.

"Is that what Metcalfe briefed you to say?" he asked at length coldly. "Don't you realise that's the whole reason I told him we'd never met? So that he wouldn't try to exploit you?"

185

"Peter wouldn't dream of suggesting such a thing. It's just that I've become ... goal-oriented. I want the play to be a success. *I* want to be a success. Just like you want me in your bed. I'm not talking about marriage – this is a straight exchange of favours. I give you what you want for as long as you give me what I want. You could do my career a lot of good, Jack. You're a very powerful man." She kept her voice deliberately cool, odiously sincere.

"You can't be serious."

"Oh, but I am. I've done a lot of thinking since Catalina. I've decided to be a winner, just like you. And you win more often with loaded dice. You taught me that, Jack."

He stepped back from her.

"Still a salesman at heart, aren't you, Carla? I liked you better when you were selling Wonderjunk. At least then you weren't selling yourself."

"Heavy moralising doesn't become you, Jack. Why be a hypocrite? We all have to survive as best we can. Well, do I make myself comfortable, or are you going to take me home?"

With icy calm, Jack took a five-pound note out of his wallet and stuffed it roughly into her hand.

"Get yourself a godammed cab," he said thickly, fighting an instinct towards violence. "And send me a bill, won't you, for our time together in Italy? I wouldn't like you thinking I didn't pay my debts. What was that Italian word that wasn't in my phrase book? Oh yes, I remember – *puttana*. I always knew it would come in useful one of these days."

His face ashen with rage, he gave her a look so full of hurt and hatred that Carla could never decide afterwards which one of them had suffered more. Then he slammed out of the room and out of her life.

Chapter Ten

"Streetwise" enjoyed a long and healthy extended run at the Gallery. By Christmas, it was still playing to packed houses. Both the prestige and the cash benefits had been a shot in the arm for the struggling theatre, but gradually they had all come to accept that there would be, after all, no West End transfer. There was vague talk of touring the provinces which, to Carla's relief, had as yet come to nothing. She had no desire to spend weeks away from home now that she and Francesca were settling in nicely in Remo's new house.

A comfortable routine had established itself whereby either Angela or Mamma would stay overnight to mind Francesca when Carla was late home from the theatre. She was always, however, at home to welcome her from school, as the Gallery didn't give weekday matinées, and although Saturday involved two consecutive performances she made a point of devoting the whole of Sunday to jointly pleasurable activities.

Not that being a mother was all sweetness and light. Francesca, for all her sunny personality, was no goody-goody and, as children will, she set out to find and test out Carla's limits. Mrs de Luca had ruled with an iron hand and it was only to be expected that Francesca would instinctively exploit Carla's relative lack of experience. But as her style of parenthood, albeit different from Mamma's, gradually asserted itself, Francesca settled down under the new régime, blossoming under the unaccustomed luxury of being suddenly an only child instead of the youngest of the litter. She had inherited Carla's tendency to be a bookworm, long thwarted by the noise, bustle and cramped conditions in the de Luca household. But now, with Carla's help, she was tackling quite sophisticated reading for her age. Her performance at school improved dramatically, as did her general maturity and self-confidence. Carla, who had been rather dreading facing the nuns on Open Day in her new role as a parent, came home fairly bursting with maternal pride after hearing glowing reports from Francesca's class teacher, and later sat through the Junior nativity play, sniffing in absurdly sentimental fashion over Francesca's deadpan rendering of the Virgin Mary.

In the long, lonely nights when she still wept over Jack, she reminded herself constantly that she had made the right decision. The cosy, stable, secure base she had been able to give her daughter already lacked nothing that money could buy. Two committed, caring parents would have been better than one, no doubt, but at least this way Francesca was the focus of what love there was. Better by far for her to be no man's child than to be relegated to the role of another man's child.

Jack Fitzgerald, Peter informed her with chagrin, had left London the day after their meeting. True to form, Peter had rung Jack's office on the following Monday to stage a last-ditch stand, only to be told that Mr Fitzgerald had gone on a long vacation, no-one knew where, and that he would therefore be incommunicado for some time. All his interests had been delegated, and if Mr Metcalfe would care to state his business, the appropriate nominee would call him right back, etc, etc. Peter, heartily cursing Carla's prudishness, had been forced to give up. But he already felt too sheepish at the crass suggestions he had made to continue to press his own attentions on Carla. Unaccountably, she had moved out to the sticks somewhere, and was oddly secretive when questioned about it. Peter, and several others, assumed that she was probably living with someone, and wanted to keep it quiet. Which in a way, of course, was quite true.

Early in the New Year, news came through that one of the television companies was interested in including an analysis of "Streetwise" in a weekly Arts slot entitled "The Contemporary Stage". This was a great morale-booster for everyone, meaning a nice fat cheque for all the cast as videoed excerpts of the play were to be shown punctuated by comments and discussion from a panel comprising Peter Metcalfe, Carla and Simon Duff which was to be presided over by Piers Simpson, a well-known TV Arts pundit. Josiah Freeman had, of course, declined to participate, for which everyone concerned was heartily relieved. His monosyllabic conversational style was hardly likely to be missed.

The filmed excerpts were a simple, low-budget affair involving two cameras and no retakes. However, the discussion, later to be edited around the clips, did not proceed so smoothly.

Piers Simpson always liked to have an angle, a particular slant on every subject, and he had decided to make a feature of Josiah Freeman's absence. Although he would not have relished the uphill work of interviewing such a man, it was in fact quite unheard of to refuse an invitation to appear on Piers Simpson's programme, generally acknowledged to be free publicity of the most advantageous sort. Could Freeman's success, Simpson asked acerbically, be simply a flash in the pan? Could it be that "Streetwise" owed more to its interpreters than to its originator? Was this play, perhaps, a one-off freak – a common enough theatrical phenomenon – a fortunate vehicle for a brilliant director and a talented cast, but fundamentally lacking in substance?

Peter Metcalfe, responding, flannelled away to the effect that this was an interesting theory but only time would tell, exhaling a great deal of hot air in his anxiety to retain as much credit for himself as possible without obviously knocking Freeman. Besides, Piers Simpson was a valuable contact and he had high hopes of featuring on future programmes.

Simon Duff, for his part, was interested only in getting in as many plugs for the Gallery as possible, and waxed extremely tedious on the need for subsidy and the iniquity of Government cuts. Meanwhile, Carla was rapidly coming to the conclusion that she had been invited along for purely decorative reasons. She hardly got a chance to say anything at all amid the constant male interruptions, and bitterly resented Piers Simpson's off-camera leers. Finally, on noticing the producer issuing 'winding up' signals, she was goaded into action.

To everyone's astonishment, she cut across Piers Simpson in full flow and, for two impassioned minutes while the other participants looked on open-mouthed, completely debunked Simpson's shallow assessment of Freeman's rôle as the play's creator. She stated in no uncertain terms that any competent band of professionals could have achieved success with a work of this calibre. She for one was confident that Freeman's next play would be even better. She also vastly admired a man whose talent was such that he did not need to pander to publicity or play up to media hype. She was disappointed that a serious programme such as this should so trivialise important issues and give the public so superficial and biased a view of what made good theatre. She hoped that the excerpts from the play would

190

speak for themselves. The orchestra was important, vitally so, but it did not compose the music.

Simpson, used to calling the tune, rose to the bait and rather unwisely argued back, with the result that the ensuing discussion became quite heated, despite Peter Metcalfe's frantic sign language to Carla to shut up. By the time the cameras had stopped rolling, it was quite clear that Carla's superior knowledge and insight had completely flattened the odious Piers Simpson. As soon as the recording was over, he stalked off in high dudgeon without a word.

Peter hissed at Carla, "For God's sake, did you have to go over the top like that? That's the last person on earth you want to fall out with. He's got a lot of influence, you silly bitch. He could put work your way – and mine!"

Simon Duff, ineffectual as ever, mumbled his excuses and made a hurried exit, unwilling to become involved in a full-scale row.

"I don't expect to be invited on to a programme like this just to provide crumpet, or to toady to a self-opinionated pseud like that," she fumed. "Just because Freeman is a mediaphobe is no reason for the rest of us to sell him short."

"Don't be bloody naive," snapped Peter, exasperated. "You don't suppose for one minute, do you, that your sanctimonious views will actually reach the pig-ignorant public? You'll be edited out of existence. What you did back there was completely gratuitous. I hope you're not starting to show signs of artistic temperament, Carla. You can't afford such luxuries yet. You've just done your career – and the play – no good at all!"

But Peter, of all people, should have known what makes good television. What got cut was his own meaningless waffle. Piers Simpson, unwilling to appear paranoid, had to agree at his producer's insistence to let

Carla's outburst go out unexpurgated, with unforeseen results.

The programme was broadcast a week later. Most of the TV reviewers picked it up for comment, ranging from 'Sock it to 'im, Carla!' in one of the more down-market Sundays, to 'The Freeman Debate Continues' in the staidest of the prestige dailies. The level of exposure Carla received led to an untypically impressed Molly phoning her to say that it looked like there was a telly play in the offing – a heavy drama set in Belfast – and a female features writer wanted to interview her.

"Colour supplement job. She's doing a weekly piece on 'Women in the Arts' or some such nonsense. Money for old rope and good publicity." Molly snorted encouragingly. "She wants to come over to your place with a photographer one morning," she continued. "Will any day do?"

"Do they have to come to my home?" asked Carla uneasily. "Couldn't we meet somewhere? At the theatre, perhaps?"

"No, no, they want the personal angle. You know the type of thing. Your tastes and life style, what you eat for breakfast, all that rubbish. She said Wednesday would be best, about elevenish. Okay with you?"

Oh well, thought Carla, she would have the house to herself, and she could hardly afford to refuse, much as she dreaded the prospect of probing questions. There was no way Molly would let her wriggle out of this one.

It was to be Carla's first experience of being interviewed, and she carefully rehearsed various little all-purpose speeches in preparation for her ordeal. She had a healthy fear of journalists. Molly, trying to reassure her, had said cheerfully that as they always distorted whatever you said, there wasn't really any point in worrying about it which well-meaning advice did nothing to improve Carla's peace of mind. She knew that Molly was right about its being free publicity. "Streetwise's" run would soon be over, and she needed to have more than one possible television play on the stocks to keep herself on an even keel financially. Regular work had spoiled her. She didn't want to go back to selling or waitressing, and that would be inevitable unless more parts came from somewhere. And nothing got you parts like having parts.

The top floor of Remo and Gabby's house, with a coat of white paint, sanded floorboards and potted plants, was still bare but starkly tasteful. On the following Wednesday morning, Carla saw Francesca off to school as usual, dusted vigorously, dressed herself with elegant casualness, and awaited her interrogator.

The journalist, Mandy Fellowes, turned out to be a rather breathy up-and-coming young reporter, not long out of Cambridge and very anxious to prove herself. She arrived on the dot of eleven, accompanied by a very bored looking lanky photographer who soon made himself at home with his newspaper and proceeded to ignore both women. Evidently the photographs were not to be taken till the interview had warmed up.

Mandy Fellowes was ambitious and intelligent enough not to have skimped on her homework, and had already researched the factual side of Carla's career through Molly. The purpose of this interview, she explained, was to examine the angle of the actress being dominated in a man's world of writers, producers and directors. What were Carla's comments on the pressures on young actresses to exploit their sex appeal rather than rely on their talent? She had been very impressed, she said, at how Carla had put Piers Simpson in his place. Not many actresses would have risked sticking out their necks so boldly when it was easier just to nod and simper. Carla rather threw discretion to the winds by endorsing most of Mandy's views about the actress as

193

sex object, and repeated how wonderful it was that writers like Josiah Freeman created female characters as real women and not just as routine love interest. Further discussion of Anna Price's personal dilemmas led Mandy on to the 'human interest' angle.

"And what are your views," she asked predictably, "on combining the stage with eventual marriage and motherhood?"

Carla had a neat little speech ready prepared to side-step this expected question but even as she opened her mouth to deliver it, she heard the latch on the front door and two pairs of feet hurtling up the stairs. Seconds later Silvana marched in with Francesca in tow. They were both giggling fit to burst and both covered in a bright pink rash.

"Sister Joseph sent us home," Silvana explained breathlessly, obviously pleased as punch. "We've caught the German measles epidemic!"

"Just look at my spots!" Francesca exclaimed, displaying herself proudly. "They weren't there when I got up this morning! There are ever so many on my tummy. But I feel all right, so I don't have to go to bed, do I?"

Before Carla could reply Mandy cut in with, "What a pretty little girl. She looks very like you. Is she your niece?"

Francesca gave Carla a brief, hesitant, testing look, as if wondering whether her mother would deny her. Instinctively she did not speak herself, looking Mandy up and down with unabashed curiosity.

"No," said Carla steadily. "This is Francesca, my daughter. She will be eight next birthday. And this is Silvana, my sister, who's eleven. Silvana, I think perhaps you'd better get off home. Francesca, you can play in your room for a bit. I'll take your temperature when this lady's gone."

The photographer, roused from his apathy, started examining Francesca through his viewfinder.

"How about a picture of you with your daughter, Miss de Luca? I can fix it so the spots won't show. I'd like some outdoor shots, if you don't mind, the light's just right."

"Terrific," enthused Mandy, doing some rapid mental arithmetic. If this child was nearly eight, she must have been born when Carla de Luca was *sixteen*! What a scoop.

Obediently, Carla and Francesca posed for the photographer, Francesca on the garden swing Remo had attached to the apple tree, with Carla pushing. Then Francesca was despatched to her room while Mandy pursued this new angle with gusto. Carla wasn't married, was she? How had she coped? How did one combine acting with single parenthood? She must have been very young when her daughter was born, had this influenced her choice of career? Etc, etc.

Carla, realising the hidden dangers of these loaded questions, took charge firmly, saying that she relied heavily on the love and support of her mother and sisters, and that if and when she ever married it would be a case of love me, love my child. Affection was more important to a child than money or possessions, and it took a very special type of man to be a good stepfather. Perhaps that was why more and more women in her position were opting to go it alone.

"Do I get to see the copy before you print it?" she asked anxiously. "I'm very concerned that you don't publish anything that could cause my daughter or my family distress."

Mandy, delighted at the success of the interview, and quite captivated by Francesca, shook her hand warmly.

"Please don't worry. I understand absolutely, and I'm one hundred per cent on your side. Thank you so much.

195

And do keep up the good work." And with a wave, they were gone.

After that, there was obviously no point in continuing to keep Francesca a professional secret. Carla's now established reputation would bely any fears that her maternal responsibilities might interfere with her commitment to her work. Because she was known to be always punctual, always reliable, always meticulous, the exposure of her well-hidden private life only served to increase the regard in which her colleagues held her. Mandy kept her word and sent Carla proofs of the article before it was due to appear. Carla squirmed a bit when she read them, but, once she cut through the rather extravagant journalese, she couldn't in conscience try to veto the copy.

"Carla de Luca's forthright professional views mirror her courage and integrity in her private life ... a single parent, Carla may be justly proud of her delightful seven-year-old daughter Francesca, who doesn't appear to have suffered in the least from lack of a father ... 'Any man I marry,' says Carla, 'must be capable of loving Francesca as if she were his own' ... Carla assures me that there are no likely candidates in view at the moment ... Somehow I feel it won't be long before some astute man sees this double package as a bargain not to be missed ..."

Rather syrupy for Carla's taste, and excessively flattering, but fundamentally accurate and obviously well-meaning. Better, as Molly wisely pointed out, than a kick in the teeth. The photograph selected was charming, mother and daughter both displaying the same unposed, gleeful smile as the swing was frozen in its downward rush.

Mamma, who had at first been horrified that the family's private affairs would soon be public, had literally lapped up the final result and bought a dozen copies.

196

"Not many girls," she pontificated to the neighbours, "got guts like my Carla."

That's one gutsy lady, mused Harvey G. Brennan, Casting Director for Phoenix Productions, Inc. An unaccustomed gleam lit up his jaded eye. Pretty girls – beautiful women, come to that – were two a penny in the movie industry. No, what he was looking for was a fiery temperament, an independent spirit, spunk, originality . . . and his budget wouldn't run to Meryl Streep.

Yet again he froze Carla's image on the video recording of the Piers Simpson show, her eyes blazing, her hands gesturing expressively. The Simpson guy, like all critics, was a jerk. Brennan liked the way Carla had put him down. He liked what he'd read about her, too. All that go-it-alone stuff projected exactly the right image. It would give the hype boys an angle to work on.

He reached for the telephone.

"Of *course* I've read 'A Place in the Sun'!" shrieked Gabriella, jumping up and down in excitement. "You mean to say you haven't?"

Carla was still stunned at Molly's telephone call. For the first time in their working relationship, her agent had actually sounded enthusiastic. Perhaps, for once, her percentage would be worth having.

"Not yet," she admitted, fingering the cover of the three-inch-thick blockbuster she'd hurriedly purchased that afternoon. "Perhaps you'd better give me a potted version of it, Gabby. I don't know if I can take all this in by tomorrow."

"A TV mini-series!" crowed Gabby rapturously, hugging her sister in delight. "Just think, Carla – today you're an unknown, tomorrow you'll be recognised by millions of viewers all over the world!"

"Steady on," said Carla mildly. "I haven't got the part yet. And even if I'm offered it, I'm not at all sure I would accept it."

Carla wasn't making a very good job of appearing diffident, thought Gabby. To a sister's eye it was perfectly obvious that she wanted the part like mad. And if she was hesitant about accepting it, that could only be for one reason.

"Don't you dare even think about turning it down," admonished Gabby sternly. "If it's Francesca you're worried about, relax. We're all here to look after her for you. Mamma will be over the moon!"

Molly had already lectured Carla at some length.

"This is your big chance, Carla," she had insisted over the phone. "Don't blow it, for God's sake. Lucky for you they're after a new face. These series make their own stars. The budget's going into the film rights and locations, not the actors, so they're getting you for peanuts in movie terms which means, incidentally, more money than we've – I mean, you've – ever made in your life. As for the location work," she'd added warningly, "don't forget that home is where the part is."

Location work. 'A Place in the Sun' was one of those sweeping global sagas, the heroine's rise to fame and fortune set against an ever-changing backdrop of East Coast, West Coast, and every major capital in Europe. Shooting would involve not just weeks but months away from home.

But of course, all this was academic. She wasn't going to get the part. She was, no doubt, one of dozens who'd been called in for testing. In any case, she didn't want the part. All she wanted was regular, reliable, home-based work. All she wanted was to provide a secure base for Francesca. That was what she had given up Jack for, wasn't it?

But unfortunately Carla did want the part. Poring

198

over the book well into the small hours, she finally gave up trying to convince herself otherwise. The action-packed story portrayed the brilliant but chequered career of Tania Forsyth, a bright and determined young secretary who plans to work her way up to executive status. Disillusioned and angered by the patronising and sexist attitudes of her male bosses, she resolves, against all the odds, to build her own business empire, a project encompassing fifteen years, a thousand pages, and six hours of television. Brave yet vulnerable, defiant yet insecure, with heart and head locked in endless combat, Tania certainly honoured the purple promises of the blurb on the cover, delivering triumph and heartbreak, love and betrayal, success and sacrifice.

Oh yes, Carla wanted the part all right. And as Gabby had rightly pointed out, of course Mamma and the girls would look after Francesca for her, willingly, lovingly. Just as they would have done while she globe-trotted with Jack . . .

Harvey Brennan was intrigued. Carla de Luca's reading of the part was by far the best he'd seen – intelligent, well thought-out, forceful, disciplined. But, unlike her rivals, she had seemed oddly subdued, indifferent even, when he had outlined the terms of any possible contract. Specifically, she appeared unmoved by the references to New York, Paris, Vienna, or the other glittering locations which made the book such good potential television.

I'm doing this deliberately, thought Carla, with helpless insight. I'm so frightened he'll offer me the job I'm sending out messages that I don't want it, even though I do. Luckily, her total, instinctive professionalism had protected her during the actual audition. She couldn't have performed badly to save her life, she had too much pride. But for one who had sold everything from Wondercrêpe to Catalina, she was strangely incapable of selling herself.

While Harvey Brennan listened, disappointed, to her vague responses, Carla found herself wondering what Tania Forsyth, the story's heroine, would do in her position. She didn't wonder long. So total had been her absorption of the character that the answer sprang forward instantly, spontaneously, surprising Carla almost as much as Harvey Brennan.

"If I were to accept this part," she heard herself saying coolly, quietly, assertively, "it would be on condition that my daughter accompanied me everywhere. Her transport, accommodation and tuition would have to be written into my contract. No part in the world is worth losing six months of my child growing up. From your point of view, of course, it would be a good investment. You'd get your moneysworth, with interest."

And then she smiled, dazzlingly, disarmingly, as if she had every confidence in Harvey Brennan's ability to meet this outrageous demand from an unknown actress, stubbornly looking her gift horse in the mouth.

While he stared at her in amused fascination, wondering if he had heard her right, Carla looked him straight in the eye and added provocatively, mock-apologetically, "I'm afraid that acting in character is an occupational hazard. But I'm sure Tania Forsyth would approve."

Molly's threats to tear Carla limb from limb were quickly forgotten once the contract was safely signed and sealed. Although shooting was not due to commence for some time, the publicity machine had already swung into action. A press reception was to be held at a big London hotel, a huge multi-purpose circus of an affair designed to boost book sales, stimulate increased investment in Phoenix Productions, promote Carla as a megastarlet, and generally pander to Fleet Street's interest in checking out free champagne.

Francesca, oblivious to all the complications, was ecstatic at the prospect of her forthcoming travels, and spent many speculative hours poring over her atlas. Meanwhile, Molly's phone never stopped ringing. Suddenly, Carla found herself in demand, and being all too aware of the ephemeral nature of success in her line of work, she resolved to make the most of it as insurance against the inevitable lean times ahead.

The reception was a new and daunting experience for her. It was preceded by a briefing from the public relations people about the likely questions journalists would ask, and a list was circulated of other guests who had been invited in deference to their creative, practical, or financial usefulness. Molly, resembling a whorehouse madam in a fur-trimmed shocking pink two-piece, kept hissing furtive advice at Carla out of the corner of her mouth like an inept ventriloquist. Her eyes scanned the list of invitees, as she muttered garbled mini-biographies of the names she recognised.

"Speak nicely to that old fool Bill Ferguson," she advised Carla belligerently. "I wangled his invite for your benefit. He masterminds those half-witted quiz shows with panels of so-called celebrities. Money for jam. Chat him up a bit, there's a good girl."

"Uh-huh," Carla murmured abstractedly, practising mental yoga for all she was worth. It was unnerving, not having any lines. This was the ultimate ad-libbing nightmare.

"Freda Firkin," continued Molly alphabetically. "Never heard of her. What a name. Jack Fitzgerald – that sounds familiar."

"What?" croaked Carla as her heart went into overdrive.

"Fitzgerald Enterprises, it says. Mmm. Probably a

money-bags guest. Dirty old men, most of them. Sam Freer . . . no, don't know him . . ."

"I must powder my nose," Carla mumbled, and disappeared.

It had to happen sooner or later, she reminded herself, breathing deeply in the plush pink privacy of the Powder Room. Sooner or later a working actress was bound to stumble across a man who regularly invested in the entertainment business. And, like everyone else on that guest list, Jack would shortly be presented with a glossy factpack, including a studio portrait of Carla and the usual one-paragraph life story, ending with the words: "and lives in London with her daughter, Francesca." Just in case he didn't know already. Everyone else did.

So what? she told herself sternly. I'm over him. I've survived without him, and I shall prosper without him. I'm my own woman now, just like Tania Forsyth. Watch this space for the new, improved Carla de Luca, who's made it all by herself and on her own terms.

It was far worse than a first night, sitting on that platform with no script to hide behind, answering the volley of questions fired from the floor. Carla employed a trusted technique of addressing herself to a friendly face in the third row.

The publicists had chosen to make a feature of the terms of Carla's contract, and this was generating considerable interest from female reporters. Superficially, Carla appeared relaxed, witty, self-assured. Inside she felt a gibbering wreck, afraid to focus her eyes on anyone for fear she would spot Jack and completely lose her cool. Perhaps he wasn't there, she told herself. Except that she knew he was. She could feel him in the air.

She heard him before she saw him. In fact the sound of his voice made her shut her eyes in a vain attempt to lessen its impact. She should have known that shutting one's eyes makes sounds seem all the more distinct.

His question was quietly spoken but clearly audible throughout the vast room.

"And how does your daughter feel, Ms de Luca," he asked, journalist-style, "about roaming the world for months on end? Won't that be rather unsettling for her? Don't children need a stable base, a regular routine? Are you being fair on her?"

You swine, thought Carla, needled, rising to the bait. Curses on all men who try to exploit the working mother's inherent sense of guilt.

"Children are much more flexible than we give them credit for," she replied firmly, smiling sunnily at her ally in the third row. "Quite apart from that, a bored mother makes for a bored child. A happy, busy, fulfilled mother is bound to be a more stimulating parent. If I left Francesca at home, she might well feel neglected. That's why I'm taking her with me. The only alternative would have been to stay at home myself, and be a martyr. And a self-sacrificing, frustrated mother can't expect to bring up a happy child. Does that answer your question?"

And then her eyes were pulled telepathically, magnetically, irresistibly, to where Jack stood alone at the far end of the room. He smiled at her slowly, knowingly, privately, in a way that made her toes tingle.

"It sure does," he said.

There was no way of escaping the extended junketing which followed, as champagne flowed freely and backs were duly slapped, and scratched, and stabbed. Carla, thanks to Molly's machinations, had just been invited, much against her inclination, to participate in one of Bill Fergusons's quiz shows. She was rapidly succumbing to a third-degree headache when, mercifully, the gathering began to disperse just as the booze finally dried up.

Relieved not to have been further approached by Jack

– not to say inadmissibly piqued – Carla made her way towards the taxi that had been ordered for her, keeping her head resolutely down just in case Jack should be lying in wait by the exit.

He wasn't. Thank God for that, she told herself, dishonestly. She got into the waiting car and let it carry her home, blinking back her tears, miserably unaware that a second taxi, in the best if hackneyed movie tradition, was keeping a follow-that-cab tail on her all the way back to Ealing.

"How dare you harass me like this," she fumed as Jack joined her on the doorstep. She fumbled crossly in her bag, mysteriously unable to locate her latchkey. "You had no right to follow me home. If you think I'm going to invite you in, I'm afraid you've got another think coming!" She held on to her anger for dear life, like a drowning man clutching at driftwood.

"Sorry you feel that way," Jack apologised mildly, "but I thought you'd appreciate my not foisting myself on you in public, especially with all those trigger-happy photographers about."

"Very discreet of you, I'm sure. You could have phoned first if you'd wanted to see me, instead of waylaying me like this."

"I wanted the advantage of surprise, Carla. Besides, I didn't want to give you the chance of hanging up on me."

"You mean you'd prefer to have the door shut in your face?"

Carla opened the front door briskly, stepped inside and stood facing him, barring his entry and trembling all over. She studiously avoided the penetrating candour of his gaze.

"Go on, then," he said softly. "Shut the door in my face."

It worked. She let him in.

Buying time, Jack asked for a cup of coffee he had no intention of drinking. Carla's hands shook as she briskly clattered together a tray.

"I suppose I went a bit over the top just now," she admitted grudgingly. "You caught me unawares and my nerves took quite a jangling at that press conference. It was rather an intimidating experience for a fringe actress like me."

"Don't worry, it didn't show," Jack observed dryly. "They were gobbling you up like candy back there. I predict you'll be flying high for a year or two until they suddenly decide it's your turn to be shot down in flames. That's when you find out how tough you really are."

"Oh, I think I'm tough enough, thank you."

He smiled cryptically. "Good, you'll need to be."

"Better to be tough than a loser," she countered defensively. "Besides, I've got Francesca to think of."

There, she'd said it. The name that stood between them.

"Oh yes, Francesca. Francesca. Boy, did you set me up nicely with that heart-rending little sob story of yours. I fell for it in a big way, didn't I, telling you how it was all for the best, what a blessing in disguise that your baby had died, how kids are a big drag anyway, how glad I was not to be saddled with another guy's bastard. I sure said all the wrong things that day, didn't I? With you busy feeding me all the cues."

"You meant every word of it. You can't deny truth with hindsight."

"Don't you dare talk to me about truth," snarled Jack with sudden savagery, giving vent to the feelings he had held so rigorously in check. "You lied to me. You punished me for being honest. You never gave me a chance. You deliberately, cold-bloodedly dug a hole and

205

watched me fall right into it. Even when I climbed out of it and came grovelling back to you in London, you pushed me straight back in. That was some performance you laid on that night, Carla. You're an actress down to your fingertips. But let's get one thing straight. Don't you ever, ever *act* with me again!"

The raw pain in his voice made her wince, but she steeled herself to bear it. There was no point in wallowing in self-indulgent regrets. One sign of weakness, and Jack would walk all over her. She couldn't risk it.

"I couldn't tell you the truth," she said defensively. "You know perfectly well why I lied to you. I did it to protect Francesca."

"More lies, damn you! You did it to protect *yourself*!"

"Stop shouting at me!"

"Thank your stars that that's all I'm doing. I've a score to settle with you, Carla. Do you seriously think I came here to let bygones be bygones? To forgive and forget? Especially forget? I've just been through the most miserable, bitter, *lonely* period of my life, all on account of you, and you complain that I'm *shouting* at you? You're lucky I'm not wringing your lying neck. You're lucky I'm not – not –"

And as Carla flinched, expecting him, almost wanting him, to lash out at her, he grabbed hold of her bodily and hugged her so tight that all the air was squeezed out of her lungs. "You are *not*," she heard him say indistinctly, "repeat, *not*, going to wriggle out of this."

Wisely, she didn't try. She didn't want to. Paradoxically, it was as if he was protecting her against himself, directing his pent-up hurt and anger into this ferocious, possessive, bone-crushing embrace, communicating his pain as a way of defusing his wrath.

Wordlessly they stood like that, immobile, rigid, Jack striving for calm, Carla searching for strength.

Don't kiss her, he told himself with difficulty. Not

yet. Medicine first, sugar later. The other way round made the medicine taste worse.

"All right," he said at last, releasing her. "You know what I want. The truth. The truth I can take, however bad it is, but I won't stand for any more lies. If you don't love me, then tell me now, right away, and I'll leave you alone and not harass you any more. But you've got to look me in the eye while you say it, and it's got to be for real. No acting. You're good, but not that good. At least, I hope not."

Carla looked away. Jack waited. Then she met his eyes.

"Still the same old Jack," she said knowingly. "You'd never have gambled that question, would you, if the dice wasn't loaded? You know perfectly well that I still love you, you bastard."

And then Jack grinned, several years dropping away from a face which had grown tired and taut. His relief was so apparent that Carla realised he'd had doubts about that dice after all. A huge wave of tenderness nearly knocked her flat. Attack, she reminded herself. Attack was the best form of defence.

"Oh yes," she continued dryly, "I love you all right. Terrific for your ego. But there's no future in it, and there never was. I never deceived you about that, especially now that I've finally begun to build a new life for myself and Francesca. I've got a lot of lost time to make up for with her. I nearly left it too late. It would have been so easy, to give in and marry you. Putting her first is the hardest thing I've ever had to do. But I'd rather she had one committed parent rather than two half-hearted ones."

"Carla, I –"

"Let me finish! I'm making out, Jack. I'm more than making out. I've got my daughter back, and I've got my career. I've done it all without you. And I'm not

207

giving it up, any of it. If you think you can come bulldozing your way back into my life and taking it over, then you're wrong. I let you dominate me once, I know, but I've come a long way since then. I've grown up, if you like. Enough to face up to my responsibilities. I can't think just of myself any more. If you had a child, you'd understand."

"Then give me one!" he interrupted, exasperated. "Give me Francesca! What makes you think I can't love her, too? I've been hoarding my love all my life, Carla, like some kind of miser. I never spent a cent of it till you came along, and there's more than enough for both of you. Stop using Francesca to try to scare me off. You're the one who's scared, not me.

"Are you worried she'll give me a hard time? I hope she does. Because the more difficult she makes it for me, the more I can prove myself. I never thought marriage to you would be *easy*, even before I knew about her. I never even wanted it to be. I enjoy risks, remember? And this time all I've loaded the dice with is love. So let her kick me in the shins and tell me she hates me – I can handle it. But don't take my word for it. Make me prove it. Watch me prove it. Let me prove it, Carla."

She felt dizzy, weak, defeated. She wasn't up to this. She was too tired to fight him. Worse, she didn't want to. She wanted to give in.

"You're a born salesman, aren't you?" she said wearily.

Jack shrugged. "It takes one to know one. The question is, will you buy? The deal is very simple. What you see is what you get. Me, as I am, for keeps. That's all. So go ahead. Argue with me. Give me one hundred good reasons why it won't work. But don't expect me to give up. This is a hard sell. The pay-off is too good to lose."

"If I said yes," said Carla, shaking her head, "I do believe you'd feel cheated."

"You're right. Say no. Go on."

He sat down and stretched out his legs, in his element now, with the sublime confidence of a man with a trick up his sleeve. But there were some things he couldn't talk his way out of, thought Carla, rising to the challenge.

"Okay then," she said grimly. "You asked for it. It's all pretty obvious stuff. One, you're not the marrying kind. Meaning you're bored by domesticity, stifled by routine, you hate being tied down to any one place."

Jack appeared to give the matter some thought.

"True," he admitted finally, with a cheerful lack of remorse.

"Two," continued Carla, "you like bright lights, excitement, variety. You like living out of suitcases, seeing new places, new people, being on the move."

Jack pondered, nodded slowly, and said, "Okay. No point denying it."

"Three," she went on relentlessly, "you live strictly for the moment. You enjoy taking risks. You refuse to plan too far in advance. Security blunts your edge."

Jack pursed his lips and considered these accusations.

"You know me pretty well, don't you?" he observed, sighing. "Well, I guess I'm too old to change my spots now."

Carla looked at him blankly. She had been expecting him to protest, to announce that it was high time he settled down and rejected his hectic life-style. She had been waiting for him to come up with all manner of pipe-and-slippers resolutions, in a bid to convince her that he could provide the kind of stability she wanted for Francesca.

"Well then," Carla said, somewhat deflated. "There's nothing left to say, is there? I told you, Francesca

209

deserves a proper home and a proper father. I can't sacrifice her needs to a purely selfish love."

"I see," said Jack ruefully. "You made your point. Is it my turn now?"

"Your turn?"

"To dish out the home truths. Fair's fair."

"Home truths?"

"Yep. Correct me if I'm wrong. A child needs a regular routine, a settled environment, a secure base."

"Yes, of course."

"And a parent's needs are always secondary to providing that?"

"Er . . . yes."

"Ms de Luca," continued Jack, journalist-style, "tell me, how does your daughter feel about travelling around with you for months on end?"

Carla opened her mouth and shut it again.

"Could it be," continued Jack mercilessly, "that children are much more flexible than people think? Could it be that she prefers a happy, busy, fulfilled mother to a self-sacrificing martyr? Could it be that—"

"Stop it!" hissed Carla. "Stop twisting my words!"

"I'm quoting you verbatim, sweetheart, and you know it. Every damn thing you've just said about me applies to you as well. Why can't you admit that? Your choice of career proves it. Even when you weren't acting, you never did a 'proper' job, did you? Never got yourself a desk and a regular paycheck? No, you've always opted to live by your wits, every bit as much as I have.

"And then look at this film. What does it offer? I'll tell you. Endless travel, crazy schedules, constant pressure. Pretty routine, huh? And of course it's a gamble, whichever way you look at it. You could end up a big star, yes, but you could be a god-awful flop or all your best scenes could end up on the cutting room floor.

There are no guarantees in show business. Terrific security, right?

"And do you know what you'll be doing this time next year? Silly question! You haven't even thought that far ahead because all you care about is what you're doing right now. And you know why? Because that's the way you like it, Carla. You're hooked on adrenalin, just like me. Stop trying to kid yourself you want a quiet, safe, well-ordered life. You don't, any more than I do. Hasn't it ever occurred to you," he demanded, seizing both her hands, "how *alike* we are?"

Alike? She and Jack? Of course they weren't alike! Carla looked for words to protest with but they wouldn't come as she realised, with a sudden flood of self-knowledge, that she had endlessly attacked the qualities in Jack which she feared to acknowledge in herself.

"But . . ." she faltered despairingly, "but . . . you're a man!"

"You mean you noticed?"

"I mean . . . oh God, all right, I've been kidding myself. I'm too selfish to be any kind of mother! I've put my career ahead of Francesca and dreamed up all kinds of ways of justifying myself to salve my conscience. I'm like all actresses – a raving egomaniac!"

"Correction. You are not like all actresses. You're different. Talented. Special. So face up to it. Don't ever apologise for it. As for Francesca – trust her, Carla. She can take it. Don't make the same mistake with her as you did with me. Have some faith in her. Never under-estimate how much she loves you."

Oh, to hell with more words, thought Jack impatiently, seeing her eyes fill with tears. He kissed her. Words were clumsy, inadequate, ambiguous, but there would be no mistaking the silent, eloquent message in his kiss. It exacted punishment even as it begged forgiveness. It was greedy yet generous, sensual yet subtle, masterful yet humble. It was Jack.

Memories flooded through her as she savoured once again the old, familiar, drugging taste of love. A long, slow moment later there was no more pain just a delicious, healing ache, no more fear just the tingle of challenge, as they stood locked together in quiet forgiveness and promised joy.

"You'll have to go now," said Carla weakly, some time later. "Francesca's due back from school any minute. I don't want you here when she gets home. I've got to think this over, Jack. Talk to her. Prepare her."

"When shall I come again, then?" he asked, forcing himself to accept this. "Tomorrow?"

Typical Jack, thought Carla, fast and furious as ever. He never wasted time winning on points if he could go for a knock-out.

"No. I need time. Don't push me. Give me a few days, at least. I'll ring you, at your office. Please, Jack."

He swallowed his frustration. He liked to make the running. He didn't want to wait for a phone call from Carla. He didn't want her to have time to change her mind. He couldn't wait to meet Francesca. But Carla had called him a bulldozer and he could be. If their partnership was to work, he'd have to learn, at long last, to back off a bit.

He nodded. "Okay," he said. "But while you're busy thinking, remember one thing. Being married to me won't be easy. Being married to me will be a really tough act. That's why you'd be so damn good at it."

And he smiled to himself knowingly. Because Carla, like himself, never bought a soft option.

Perversely, Carla sat back and waited for Jack to defy her request and call her. She had recently installed an answering machine, otherwise she would have undoubtedly sat broodingly over the telephone, waiting for it to ring. Lots of people left their messages after the tone. But there wasn't a word from Jack.

At first she was despondent – presumably he had better things to do. And then she was piqued – he must be playing hard to get, damn him. And then, belatedly, she was enlightened – he was paying her a compliment.

For the first time in his life, it was Jack who was waiting for the phone to ring. He hadn't liked it, and neither, in a way, had Carla. But it did them both good.

"You open the door, darling," said Carla, taking a deep breath as the doorbell rang. Francesca scampered off downstairs while Carla finished setting the table. This would undoubtedly be the first time Jack had ever eaten fish fingers for lunch, especially with the unlikely accompaniment of Mamma's home-made tagliatelle. But as Francesca's guest, he would have to eat her choice of dish, including the strawberry jelly and ice cream which were to follow.

Carla watched apprehensively from the top of the stairs.

"Hello," said her daughter, flinging the door wide open and sizing up her visitor. "I'm Francesca."

"Pleased to meet you, ma'am," said Jack gravely, bending to shake her hand. "I'm Jack."

Being quite unused to children, Jack simply treated Francesca as a little adult, entranced at the sight of his beloved Carla in miniature and responding to her ingenuous charm as predictably as she did to his own infinitely more sophisticated variety. Soon Carla began, much to her amusement, to feel almost superfluous. After lunch, Francesca dragged Jack off to help her do a new jig-saw – her current passion – sternly instructing him to find all the straight pieces first.

Resolutely, Carla stayed behind in the kitchen, making unnecessary quantities of soup and shortcrust pastry for the sake of keeping herself occupied. Finally she succumbed to temptation and peeped through the chink in the door to see how things were progressing. Jack was sitting cross-legged on the floor, facing her daughter, the completed jig-saw pushed to one side. Francesca had produced a pack of playing cards and they were both totally engrossed in their game. But they weren't playing snap, or even whist. The large pile of matches Francesca was gleefully claiming proved that she had taken to poker in a big way.

Quietly, Carla crept into her bedroom and set herself to learn some lines. Minutes ticked by, hours passed. She could hear low voices, occasional laughter, the odd triumphant shriek, but mostly just companionable silence. As the hands of her watch moved round to five o'clock, she started as Francesca put her head round the door. Her face was animated, her eyes shining.

"It will be all right, won't it," she asked her mother coaxingly, "if Jack stays for tea?"

Also available from Woman's Weekly Fiction

Jean Chapman
The Bellmakers

Forced to take on her pedlar grandfather's tally round and sell stockings to save her family from starvation, Leah Dexter is unprepared for the abuse and prejudice she encounters travelling alone on the new railway. And when she arrives at the village of Soston just as brothers Ben and Nat are reclaiming the cursed Monk's Bell, the superstitious local folk take her appearance as an evil omen.

When Ben intervenes to save her he wins Leah's everlasting gratitude and heart. But prejudice, superstition and the unbridled lust of the squire's son still threaten the proud and beautiful pedlar girl and those she loves...

Mary Williams

The Bridge Between

From the moment she arrives in the tiny Cornish fishing village of Port Todric in 1904, Julia Kerr loves the place. Through the ups and downs of her own writing career and her marriage to a man who always puts his painting first, she draws strength and encouragement from the unchanging rhythm of village life.

Julia's daughter Sarah, while very different from her mother, shares the same passionate wilfulness. Will she break Julia's heart by continuing to estrange herself from her family after a quarrel? Or will their shared love for the village bring about a reconciliation?

A warm and realistic love story with a lovingly rendered Cornish background, *The Bridge Between* is a book to touch the heart.

Rose Boucheron
Promise of Summer

It is 1939 and despite the threat of war the future is bright for three South London girls. While Sarah's dreams of fame propel her into a world far removed from her family and friends, her schoolfriend Julie stays closer to home, taking a clerical job in a paper factory. There she soon wins a new admirer Andrew, a RAF pilot officer and the boss's son.

Andrew's sister Olivia is also in love – with a married man – and is forced to conceal her true feelings and agree to her lover's demand for secrecy. But can she really be content to win her own happiness at the expense of another woman's?

A rich and satisfying story woven from the lives of three very different girls, hoping to secure love and futures for themselves despite the heartbreak of war.

Further titles available from Woman's Weekly Fiction

While every effort is made to keep prices low, it is sometimes necessary to increase prices at short notice. Mandarin Paperbacks reserves the right to show new retail prices on covers which may differ from those previously advertised in the text or elsewhere.

The prices shown below were correct at the time of going to press.

☐ 1 86056 000 8	**A Place in the Sun**	Nina Lambert	£1.99
☐ 1 86056 005 9	**The Bellmakers**	Jean Chapman	£1.99
☐ 1 86056 010 5	**The Bridge Between**	Mary Williams	£1.99
☐ 1 86056 015 6	**Promise of Summer**	Rose Boucheron	£1.99
☐ 1 86056 020 2	**Tallie's War**	Jan Webster	£1.99
☐ 1 86056 025 3	**Time Will Tell**	June Barraclough	£1.99
☐ 1 86056 021 0	**Lucky Star**	Betty Paul	£1.99
☐ 1 86056 055 5	**With This Ring**	Jean Saunders	£1.99
☐ 1 86056 065 2	**A Captain's Lady**	Jennifer Wray Bowie	£1.99
☐ 1 86056 060 1	**Lily's Daughter**	Diana Raymond	£1.99

All these books are available at your bookshop or newsagent, or can be ordered direct from the address below. Just tick the titles you want and fill in the form below.

Cash Sales Department, PO Box 5, Rushden, Northants NN10 6YX.
Fax: 0933 414000 : Phone 0933 414047.

Please send cheque, payable to 'Reed Book Services Ltd', or postal order for purchase price quoted and allow the following for postage and packing:

£1.00 for the first book: £1.50 for **two books or more per order.**

NAME (Block letters) ....

ADDRESS ....

.... Postcode...

☐ I enclose my remittance for £........................

☐ I wish to pay by Access/Visa Card Number

☐☐☐☐☐☐☐☐☐☐☐☐☐☐☐☐

Expiry Date ☐☐☐☐

☐ If you do not wish your name to be used by other carefully selected organisations for promotional purposes please tick this box.

Signature ....
Please quote our reference: 3 503 500 C

Orders are normally dispatched within five working days, but please allow up to twenty days for delivery.

Registered office: Michelin House, 81 Fulham Road, London SW3 6RB

Registered in England. No. 1974080